A Residue of Hope

Also by Tom Milton
Blind in Granada
A Contrite Heart
Milos and Amira
The Lost Summer
The Lineman
The Last Resort
The Godmother
Eden Valley
The Silver Locket
Orphans of War
Invisible Wounds
Leave of Absence
Outside the Gate
The Golden Door
Sara's Laughter
A Shower of Roses
Infamy
All the Flowers
The Admiral's Daughter
No Way to Peace

A Residue of Hope

Tom Milton

NEPPERHAN PRESS, LLC
YONKERS, NY

Published by Nepperhan Press, LLC
P.O. Box 1448, Yonkers, NY 10702
nepperhan@optonline.net
nepperhan.com

PUBLISHER'S NOTE
This is a work of fiction. Names, characters, places, and incidents
are the product of the author's imagination or are used fictitiously,
and any resemblance to actual persons, living or dead, events, or
locales is entirely coincidental.

Printed in the United States of America

Library of Congress Control Number:: 2023934074

ISBN 978-1-7377413-5-0

Cover art was licensed from Publitek, Inc.

For Marie

The time for flowers has passed
and we are left with each other
the hard and the soft of it
I am your mother
nothing else is clear
between you and me.

"Poem for Jessica" by Nicolette Stasko

Yonkers, 2021

ONE

MARIKA WAS POUNDING a thin slice of chicken breast in a folded sheet of plastic wrap when suddenly the landline phone rang. Holding the mallet, she stepped toward the phone, which was on the counter, and she read its screen. She didn't recognize the number, but it didn't look like a robocall so she picked up the phone and answered it.

"This is Sargent Ramírez of the Yonkers police," a woman said. "Could I please speak with Mrs. Bonetti?"

"Speaking," she said, bracing herself.

"Are you the mother of Jessica Bonetti?"

"Yes, I am. What happened?" she asked, fearing the worst.

"I don't know what happened," the woman said, "but she's in the emergency room at St. John's Riverside Hospital, where the EMS took her about ten minutes ago."

"Oh, my God. Thanks for calling," she managed to say before turning the phone off.

She put the chicken into the refrigerator and, grabbing her keys and pocketbook, she rushed out to the driveway and got into her car. She drove out onto Bellevue Place and turned left onto Park Avenue and then right onto Roberts Avenue, which took her down the hill to North Broadway, where she headed north. The hospital was a half mile away.

She turned into the entrance and into the visitors' lot, where luckily she found a place to park. Aside from having her babies there, she had come to the hospital many times over the years on visits to her father and later to Jessica, a frequent flier. Before getting out of the car she opened her pocketbook and found a mask and put it on. It was more than a year since the covid epidemic began, and though they now had vaccinations it was still infecting and killing people.

Quickly she walked from the lot to the entrance of the hospital, stopped at the reception window to show the man her vaccination card, and strode to the elevator that would take her down to the emergency room. The elevator took forever to arrive at the main floor, but it finally did, and she stepped aside while people got out. She got into the elevator and pressed the floor of the emergency room. As she descended she prayed silently with her eyes closed, beginning as usual: "Lord, please strengthen my faith, renew my hope, and deepen my love."

When she got out she proceeded directly to the reception window and told the attendant: "I'm here to see my daughter, Jessica Bonetti."

"Bonetti," the young woman repeated, looking at a computer screen. "Oh, yeah. I'll let the doctor know you're here."

"Can you tell me anything about her condition?" Marika asked, knowing the answer but asking anyway. The attendant could have been one of her students.

"I'm sorry, I can't. Please sit down and wait for the doctor. He'll be right with you."

"Okay. Thanks." She turned from the window and went to the row of plastic chairs where spouses or parents or friends of patients were despondently sitting, many of them with their eyes glued to smartphones. Sitting down, she took her own phone out of her pocketbook and tapped the number of her husband.

Frank answered after one ring as if he sensed that something had happened.

"Jessica's in the emergency room at St. John's," she told him.

"What?" He sounded alarmed though not surprised. "What happened to her?"

"I don't know. I'm waiting for a doctor to tell me."

"You don't know anything?"

"No. I'll let you know as soon as I do."

"How did she get there?"

"The EMS. The police called to let me know. They must have been at the scene of the accident."

"Did they say it was an accident?"

"No. But I don't want to think about what else it could have been."

For a while Frank was silent, probably thinking about what else it could have been, and then he said: "I'm on my way there."

"Where are you coming from?"

"White Plains. Depending on traffic, I should be there within a half hour."

"Okay. I should know something by then."

She put away her phone and sat there, staring at the floor. She had last seen Jessica two days ago when they had dinner at a pub in Hastings. It had been just the two of them because Frank was at a planning board meeting in Tarrytown, presenting an environmental impact statement for a housing project. The semester had ended, and having posted her own grades she checked to see how Jessica had done on the courses she was taking in the master's program for early childhood education. It felt as if someone punched her in the stomach when she saw that Jessica had gotten FW's in all her courses. An FW meant not only that Jessica had failed but also that she had stopped attending early in the semester, though when she was asked how she was doing in her courses she always said she was doing fine. So as much as Marika was saddened by her daughter's grades she was angered by her daughter's lies.

After they had ordered dinner instead of confronting Jessica she tried to get to the bottom of the problem by asking: "What happened this semester?"

With eyes fixed on her drink Jessica said: "I don't know. I just couldn't focus on my courses."

As a college professor Marika knew how students in their teens and early twenties might not be able to focus on their courses, but Jessica was thirty-two and by now she should have had the discipline to focus on courses that certainly weren't rocket science. "What's distracting you?"

Jessica shrugged. "I don't know."

"Is it your job?"

"No, it's not my job," Jessica said, shaking her head.

Marika believed this because her daughter had been working as a nursing assistant for eleven years and doing well at that job. It hadn't been the plan for her to work as a nursing assistant for so long, the plan had been for her to get a bachelor's degree in nursing at St. Catherine College, but after doing well for three semesters she stopped attending her courses and dropped out of the nursing program. In the fall of that year she enrolled in the nursing assistant program at Cochran School of Nursing, did well in her courses, and began this job with the plan of going back to college and resuming the program in nursing. "Is it your social life?"

"No, it's not my social life."

From what Marika knew about her daughter's social life it was mostly people she met on the internet who preyed on her weaknesses and took advantage of her. This was an issue they had tried to resolve with Jessica's therapist, whose name was Ellen. "Then what is it?"

Jessica sighed. "I don't know. I mean, I don't feel like doing anything."

"Well, maybe you should talk with Ellen."

"I don't want to talk with Ellen," Jessica said, raising her voice and finally looking up from her drink with roiled eyes. "She can't do anything for me."

"Well, she can't if you don't want to be helped."

Jessica said nothing, she only took a long sip of her drink.

"Now, what about the master's program? Do you still want to be a teacher?"

"Yeah, I think so. I just don't know if I can do those courses."

"But you've done courses that were much more challenging. So what's the problem with those courses?"

"I don't know. I guess there isn't a problem with them. There's a problem with me."

Marika paused. "Can you tell me what it is?"

"I don't know what it is. I only know there's a problem."

"Mrs. Bonetti?" a man said. It was a man with glasses and gray hair in a white lab coat, standing in front of her.

"Yes," she said, returning to the present.

"I'm Dr. Elliot. I'll take you to your daughter."

"Is she all right?" she said, getting up. Like everyone else in the hospital the doctor was wearing a mask, so she was only able to read his eyes, which didn't tell her much.

"She's going to be all right, but right now she needs all the attention we can give her."

Marika followed him past a gurney with a patient on it, lying on her back and looking wiped out. The doctor parted a curtain for her and led her into a station where she saw Jessica on a bed, connected to a ventilator, a monitor, and several lines.

"She's in a coma," the doctor said. "But she's stabilized."

Marika went to her daughter, who looked as if she was asleep, and gently laid a hand on her shoulder, saying a prayer. "What happened to her?"

"An overdose."

"An overdose of what?"

"Fentanyl," the doctor said.

Marika knew about fentanyl. From random conversations with her students she knew about the perils they could encounter, and though she was aware of the fact that Jessica dabbled in soft drugs, she had never imagined that Jessica might be taking hard drugs. "Where did she get it?"

"That's what the police would like to know. They only have the address where the EMS picked her up—because when they got there she was alone."

"What's the address?"

The doctor told her.

It was a bad area near Ashburton Avenue. One of her aunts had lived there when it had been a decent, affordable area for people who worked at the carpet factory, so Marika had been there years ago. "The police must know who lives there."

"No one lives there. The building was abandoned because of a fire, so there's no record of the person she was with."

"But someone called the EMS."

"Yes, that's their only lead. And maybe they'll be able to trace the call."

Marika stroked the forehead of her daughter, saying: "We love you, so please hang in there."

"Now that she's stabilized," the doctor said, "we're going to move her to the ICU, where they have a bed for her."

"How long will she be there?"

"As long as it takes."

She was following the gurney to the elevator when Frank appeared, evidently having been directed to them by the young woman at the reception window. His face was somber, and at the sight of Jessica he gasped. "Is she all right?"

"She's going to be all right," Marika said, repeating what the doctor had told her.

"Thank God," he said, putting an arm around her shoulder and making her realize how much she needed comforting.

While they walked to a separate elevator that would take them to the floor where the ICU was, she told him as much as she knew about what had happened.

"Well, if she was with someone," Frank said, "then it was an accident."

She hadn't reached this conclusion on her own, but she did now. "Yeah, I don't think she would have done it deliberately if she was with someone."

"Fentanyl, shit. Do you think she even knew what it was?"

"She might not have. I had a student who thought he was taking heroin but it was fentanyl, or cut with fentanyl, which is cheaper than heroin."

"What was she doing with people who take that kind of drug?"

"I have no idea. We don't even know who she was with."

"Whoever it was, I hope the police find him," he said with anger, "and put him away."

She noted his assumption that the provider of the drug was a man, but she doubted it was, based on Jessica's lack of relationships with men. More likely, it was a woman she had met on the internet pretending to be gay.

By the time they got there Jessica was already settled in an ICU room which had one other patient, an elderly woman. Jessica was still on a ventilator, and she still looked as if she was asleep. They went to her bedside where Frank reached out and touched her forehead tenderly, saying: "I love you."

Jessica would have usually said "I love you too," but now she was silent, breathing audibly and regularly. Was anything going on in her mind? Would she remember what happened to her? Would she learn from this experience?

The nurse, a woman in her mid-forties, approached them and said: "She's doing well, but we're monitoring her closely so if anything happens we'll be right on it."

"How long will you keep her on the ventilator?" Marika asked.

"Until she can breathe without assistance. But as I said, she's doing well."

They stayed until the nurse indicated that their time was up, and before leaving, Marika put a hand on her daughter's arm and said another prayer.

Back home, she resumed the task of preparing dinner while Frank sat at the kitchen table, having cracked open a can of IPA which he drank from directly. She took the chicken out of the refrigerator, she pounded two more pieces of it, and then on the counter she set a dish with flour, a bowl with an egg, and a dish with breadcrumbs.

Frank broke the silence, saying: "I think she should come home and live with us, at least until she's fully recovered."

"I agree," she said, taking some potatoes out of the colander. Jessica was living by herself in a studio apartment in Greystone. She had moved there shortly after covid overwhelmed the hospital where she was working as a nursing assistant. They were helping her pay the rent, but the plan was for her to complete a master's degree in early childhood education and get a job as a teacher, so she could become financially independent. She had done well in the program, getting A's in her courses, and this would have been her last semester.

"Do you think it was someone she met on the internet?"

"Oh, yeah. How else does she meet people?" Marika said, peeling a potato.

"She meets people at work."

"Yeah. But she also gets into trouble with them." Marika was thinking of the woman who claimed that an orderly had sexually assaulted her, whose side Jessica had taken. It turned out that the woman was lying because she had something against the orderly, and she was dismissed by the hospital. But instead of letting the matter go, Jessica persisted in defending the woman to the point where she got on the shitlist of her manager, who started giving her awful schedules. Luckily, that manager had moved on, and Jessica was in the good graces of the present manager, who had gone out of her way to accommodate her for the courses she was taking in the master's program.

"It's too bad things didn't work out with Lola," Frank said. "From what I saw of her, she seemed okay."

Lola was a coworker, a nursing assistant, who had an apartment over near Saunders Trades & Technical High School on the second floor of a two-family house in a good neighborhood. Jessica began hanging out with Lola about five years ago, and it looked as if she finally had a friend whom she had met in person. Lola, whose family was from El Salvador, expanded Jess's horizons on Latino culture and Latino food, introducing her to places in Queens where she otherwise would never have ventured. Lola's apartment had two bedrooms, and when the other woman left to get married she offered the empty apartment to Jessica, who at the age of twenty-seven should have been ready to function outside the security of her family. For a while it looked as if Jessica was successfully making the transition, but then a boyfriend of Lola moved into the apartment, and after a few rounds of verbal exchanges the conflict between Jessica and the boyfriend erupted into a physical fight in which Jessica, for all her training in karate, suffered more damage than the boyfriend. That had been the reason for her previous visit to the emergency room.

Having sliced the potatoes into pieces and mixed them in a stainless-steel bowl with olive oil and salt, Marika cut up a zucchini and put it into a skillet with olive oil, salt, and pepper. "Lola was bisexual, and that was the problem."

"You mean Jessica didn't know she was bisexual?"

"How would she have known? I mean, she has almost no experience in relationships with real people. At times I think she's confused about her own sexual identity."

"I think she is," Frank said. "But how did she get confused about it?"

"I have no idea," Marika said. "And even her therapist can't get to the bottom of it."

"I keep asking myself what we did wrong. And I know we weren't perfect parents, but I don't see what we did to confuse her about her sexual identity."

"I don't either." She put the potatoes on a baking sheet with parchment paper on it, which she slid into the hot oven. She set the timer for twenty minutes.

"Nina isn't confused about her sexual identity."

"No, she isn't," Marika agreed, sitting down while the potatoes roasted. Their younger daughter Nina was exuberantly straight, though she had finally limited herself to one boyfriend at a time. "How could our daughters be so different?"

"I don't know. They must have been born that way."

Indeed, there were physical differences. Jessica was solid, with blond hair and blue eyes from the Polish side of the family, and Nina was lithe, with dark hair and dark eyes from the Italian side. And they had behaved differently from birth. Jessica had been a difficult baby, and Nina had been a mother's dream. But saying they must have been born that way let their parents off the hook, and Marika resisted being let off the hook. "Maybe they were, but we must have affected them somehow."

"I'm sure we did. But maybe all we did was moderate their natural tendencies."

"Yeah, maybe. At least Jessica isn't in prison and Nina isn't pregnant."

"Thank the Lord," Frank said.

"They have angels watching out for them."

"And also parents watching out for them."

Marika sighed. "So what are we going to do with Jessica?"

"We're going to have her come home and live with us," Frank said steadily, "and we're going to have her see Ellen."

"Okay. But the last time I talked with her she didn't want to see Ellen."

"Well, maybe almost killing herself will change her mind about that." Frank took a sip of beer and wiped his mouth with the back of his hand. "The sad thing is, Jessica has so many good qualities, but she keeps self-destructing."

"She doesn't care about herself. She cares about others, but not about herself."

"If she cares about others, she should care about herself if for no other reason than not to hurt others." He paused. "Though I must admit that when I was young I did things that would have hurt my parents if they'd ever found out."

"I did too," she said. "And my parents never found out, but with Jessica we always find out."

"Do you think she wants us to find out?"

"Yeah. And what does that tell us?"

"It tells us she wants help."

"She needs help, but I don't know if she wants it. If she did, she'd want to see Ellen."

Frank was silent for a while, and then he said: "Well, when she recovers she might realize how lucky she is to be alive, and then she might want help."

At that point the timer went off. Marika got up, and leaving the potatoes in the oven she turned on the flame under the skillet and poured some extra light olive oil into the pan. She waited for the pan to get hot enough, and then she dipped a flattened piece of chicken into the flour, into the egg, and into the breadcrumbs, and placed it into the skillet. Since there was room she added another piece of chicken. She was following instructions from Frank's mother, who had taught her how to cook Italian food. She had come into the marriage knowing how to cook Polish food, and though Frank liked it on festive occasions he preferred Italian food on a daily basis. So tonight she was cooking chicken Milanese.

When dinner was ready she set the plates on the kitchen table and got herself a glass of white wine. By then Frank had a glass of red wine, and as usual they ate dinner at the kitchen table. For a while they talked about subjects other than Jessica, with the main focus on the covid epidemic, which had affected everyone they knew. It had especially affected Marika's students, who had lost their jobs in retail stores, hotels, and restaurants, and who lived in extended families where the virus spread from generation to generation, often killing grandparents.

Inevitably they returned to the subject of Jessica, renewed their intentions to have her see Ellen, and agreed that if there was any consolation in what had happened to their daughter it was their belief that she hadn't deliberately taken an overdose.

As usual Frank went to sleep by the count of ten after lying down, and as usual Marika lay awake for a long time, tonight for an especially long time worrying about Jessica's condition. The doctor had said she was going to be all right, but from her own experience she knew that sometimes doctors were wrong about the condition of their patients. And what if he was wrong? What if Jessica never went off the ventilator? What if she spent the rest of her life in a coma? Or what if during the night she died? Marika coped with these worries by praying to the Blessed Mother and begging for intercession.

Her thoughts then moved to the question of why Jessica kept repeating behaviors that got her into trouble. She remembered discussing this question with Ellen, who had started treating Jessica many years ago. To help Marika understand her daughter's situation Ellen had used the image of a rotary, or a traffic circle that cars entered, went around, and then exited on the road that would take them where they wanted to go. There were no rotaries where Marika had lived, so the image wouldn't have helped her if she hadn't encountered a rotary when they went to Cape Cod for two weeks every August, starting when Jessica was nine and ending when she was sixteen.

In their first year they drove to the Cape on a Saturday, the worst day for traffic because that was when the week began for people renting vacation places, and they had been on the road for more than six hours when they finally made it across the Bourne Bridge, which alone took more than an hour. Frank was driving, and as they entered a rotary he asked her to watch for Route 6, the main highway that would take them east to the town of Dennis. She leaned forward and scanned the signs for Route 6, afraid that she would miss it, but then she spotted it and told him it was the next right. And that experience helped her understand what it was like for Jessica in a mental rotary, going round and round, always taking the wrong road when she got off, and then having to get back onto the rotary, over and over. So once again in getting off the rotary Jessica had taken the wrong road and gone to that apartment near Ashburton Avenue to meet whoever had given her the fentanyl.

As she lay there sleepless Marika let her mind wander from the rotary after the Bourne Bridge to what had happened their first summer at the Cape. It cost a lot to rent a house there during the prime weeks of summer, but she and Frank wanted to give their children an experience that they would happily remember. It was an experience that their own parents couldn't afford to give them, and it was barely affordable for her and Frank, but they hoped it would be good for the girls, especially for Jessica, who during that spring was put on probation at school.

The house they rented was on a road that led to the beach, and it had a pool as well as a yard with plenty of room for children to play. The pool was filled with salt water, so it didn't need chlorine, and the lawn was level and perfectly trimmed. When they finally arrived it was late afternoon, and as soon as they had put their things away they headed for the beach to watch the sunset. It took them less than ten minutes to walk there, meeting cars of families who were leaving now and going home. The beach was on the bay, and the sun was low in the sky over Boston, casting long shadows over the sand. They took off their shoes and socks, and holding them waded into the water. They stood and watched the sun change into a red ball and slowly sink in the darkening clouds. Marika gave thanks for their being together as a family.

Later, while she was becoming familiar with the kitchen and the girls were figuring out how to use the entertainment system, Frank went to get a pizza at a place they had seen on 6A, and when he returned the girls were already watching something on television. They ate the pizza at the kitchen counter—it had sausage, which everyone liked—and then the girls went back to the television while she and Frank did the dishes. Since she liked white wine and he liked red, he opened a bottle for each of them, and they took their glasses out to the patio where there were comfortable outdoor chairs. The night was quiet, and a cool breeze was blowing from the bay, so it was pleasant on the patio, and they enjoyed a time of peace.

The next morning they slept late because they were on vacation, and Frank went out and bought coffee and a box of mixed donuts from a place on 6A. Luckily, the girls had different preferences for donuts, so there was no conflict between them, and while they sat at the kitchen table Marika made a list of groceries they would need, with a plan to go shopping in the afternoon. Around ten they headed for the beach in their swimsuits, carrying towels to lie on and a tote bag with bottles of water. It was a mild summer morning, and as they retraced their steps from last evening Marika was gladdened by the sight of roses and hydrangeas in yards of the houses they passed.

When they arrived at the beach there were already a lot of people deployed on the sand with chairs and umbrellas. The tide was lower now, with the edge of the sand extending farther out into the bay, and when they found a spot that hadn't been claimed she spread their towels side by side while the girls, accompanied by Frank, scampered toward the water. Since the beach was on the bay there were no breakers, only gentle waves, so there was nothing to deter Jessica from charging right into the ocean. Nina, holding her father's hand, was more cautious, going into the water a step at a time. With Jessica leading the way they went out more than a hundred feet from shore, and the water still hadn't reached the level of Jessica's knees.

Marika followed them, keeping an eye on Jessica, who kept going out as if she intended to walk to Boston. When the water was finally above her knees she plunged into the ocean, going under and making a fishtail splash with her feet. She had learned to swim in the pool of a neighbor, in deeper water, so Marika didn't worry about her, though she still kept an eye on her because you never knew what Jessica would do next. Emerging vigorously from the ocean, she looked as if she had been freshly baptized into a world of ultimate bliss.

Meanwhile, still holding her father's hand, Nina had ventured to a point where the water was almost to her knees, and she stopped there, content. Marika caught up with them and stayed with Nina while Frank went out and joined Jessica. For a while she watched them swim around and then with Nina holding her hand she walked back out of the water to their towels, where they sat down and enjoyed the benign warmth of the sun.

A while later as Jessica was coming out of the water she stopped to watch a boy playing with what looked like a small surfboard. He waited at the edge of the beach for a suitable wave, and then running he laid down the board and jumped on it and glided over the surface of the water for as long as possible. Intrigued, Jessica watched him take several rides, and then she said something to her father, who was standing with her. When he nodded his head Marika understood that he had agreed to buy such a board for Jessica, so that afternoon on the way back from buying groceries at the supermarket they stopped at a store that sold equipment for the beach, and Frank bought a board for Jessica. He offered to buy one for Nina, but she wasn't interested. What she really wanted was a pair of thongs with pink straps, which Frank happily bought for her.

They had ham sandwiches for lunch, and then Jessica wanted to go back to the beach and try her board. Marika let Frank take her, having had enough beach for that day, and she stayed behind in the house with Nina, who wanted to shower and wash her hair. They spent the rest of the afternoon in the kitchen, where among other things Marika cooked sauerkraut the Polish way, with fatback, onions, a bay leaf, and a pinch of sugar, letting it simmer in a covered pot for more than two hours. She had bought hotdogs at the supermarket, and you couldn't eat a hotdog without kapusta.

When Frank and Jessica returned from the beach three hours later Jessica was glowing, and she said she had the best time in her whole life. Marika was happy for her, and she hoped that having the board to play with would keep her out of trouble.

For dinner that evening Frank cooked hamburgers on the outdoor grill. Jessica liked cheese on hers, while Marika and Nina liked lettuce and tomato and Frank liked a pure and simple burger. They ate at the table on the patio, and then while the girls watched television Marika and Frank remained on the patio, drinking wine and assessing the day. They agreed that things were off to a good start, and they looked forward to the days ahead.

Toward the end of their first week, as Jessica was merrily gliding on her board, two boys stopped in front of her, blocking her way. Marika could see them but couldn't hear them. Evidently the boys were contesting her right to play on that section of the beach, and Jessica was arguing back at them. Sensing what would happen, Marika sprung up from her towel and rushed toward them, but before she got there one of the boys pushed Jessica and in retaliation Jessica punched him in the face, hard enough to knock him over. He was groggily getting up when Marika got there, in time to stop the other boy from expanding the fight. Within a few minutes a woman who must have been the injured boy's mother arrived on the scene and in a thick Boston accent castigated Jessica for hitting her son.

"She shouldn't have hit him," Marika said, "but he started it."

"My son didn't do anything," the woman said.

"Yeah, he did. I saw him push her."

"I'm calling the police."

"Go ahead and call them. I'll tell them what happened, and they'll put your son in jail where he belongs."

"You do that, bitch," the woman said.

"You should teach your son not to pick on girls, especially

when it's two against one. Come on, Jess," she told her daughter. "Let's get away from these people."

Jessica obediently picked up her board and started walking away from them.

When they were about halfway to their towels, Marika said: "You shouldn't have hit him."

"He started it. He pushed me, and he called me a loser."

Jessica was on probation for hitting a boy who had called her a loser, so this was a recurrent issue. "But you're not a loser, so that shouldn't have hurt you."

"Well, it did hurt me," Jessica said.

"I'm sorry," Marika told her, putting an arm around her. "When I was your age we used to say 'Sticks and stones can break my bones, but names can never hurt me.' So next time someone calls you a name, remember that."

"Okay. I will."

"Of course he shouldn't have pushed you, and he shouldn't have called you a name, but you shouldn't have hit him. It's never right to hit a person."

"Even if he's an asshole?"

"Yeah. Even if he's an asshole."

Jessica laid her board down next to her towel and sat down, inspecting her hand.

"Did you hurt your hand? Let's see it."

Jessica showed her a hand with skin roughly scraped on the knuckles.

"Does it hurt when you wiggle your fingers?"

"No. It's just a little sore."

"Well, next time you go on your board I'll ask your father to stand by."

As if he had been summoned Frank appeared at that moment, dripping wet from his daily swim. "Did I miss something?"

"Yeah. Jessica got into a fight with a boy. He started it, but she punched him."

"Oh, Jess," Frank said with heartache.

"I'm sorry," Jessica said. "I didn't mean to spoil our vacation."

"You haven't spoiled our vacation," Marika said. "But please don't do anything like that again. Okay?"

"Okay. I promise I won't."

After examining Jessica's hand Frank said: "You must have really walloped him."

"She did," Marika said. "She knocked him over."

"Well, I bet he's a Red Sox fan," Jessica said in her defense.

"He probably is," Frank said. "But that doesn't justify hitting him. And it doesn't justify hating him. I mean, he can't help being a Red Sox fan."

On that note they made peace, and there were no further incidents to mar their vacation.

Remembering that incident she thought about what they had done to help Jessica learn to manage her anger, but eventually she went beyond the question of anger management to the question of where the anger came from. She wasn't conscious of a source of anger within herself. She had never lost her temper with her husband or with her children. And when she did feel anger, it was only like the anger at her sister Julia for making a mess of the bedroom they shared while they were growing up. Yes, she had been angry at Julia, but she had never hit her, and Julia had never hit her. So she didn't think the anger in Jessica came from her, and she was sure it didn't come from Frank, whose only outbursts were to curse the Yankees for leaving men on base.

So where did Jessica's anger come from? Was it something she was born with? Or was it something at a deeper level that only expressed itself as anger? Was it the feeling of being a loser? Was it the feeling that drove young males, who must have felt they were losers, to take weapons and massacre children in schools? But why did they feel they were losers? Why, with so much going for her, did Jessica feel she was a loser?

TWO

AT SEVEN-THIRTY the next morning since it looked like a nice day Marika took her coffee and a bran muffin out to the deck behind the house. Frank was upstairs working remotely in the office he had set up in an empty bedroom last year when things closed down because of covid. They planned to go to the hospital as soon as visitors were allowed.

From the deck she had a view of their backyard, which on the far side had a bed of flowers that she had planted and over to the right a bed of herbs that Frank had planted. A rabbit was grazing on the lawn, nibbling clover, ears erect. The swing that used to be in the yard was gone with the children, though the spot where it had stood was marked by a darker patch of grass.

When she and Frank had moved here thirty-five years ago they believed it would be a good place to raise children. The house was in a middle-class neighborhood with a nearby shopping area, a nearby church, and a nearby elementary school. It should have been a better place for children than the urban working-class neighborhood where she had grown up, living in an apartment building with five other families.

In raising her children Marika had tried to be like her own mother, who she felt had been a perfect mother. She didn't feel that she herself had been a perfect mother, but what exactly had she done wrong? Had she expected too much of Jessica? Had she failed to accept Jessica for not being the daughter she would have wanted? Beset with these questions she felt like she was on a rotary not knowing where to get off, and in this predicament she could imagine how Jessica might feel.

She took a bite of the muffin and chewed it, followed by a sip of coffee. She remembered Frank suggesting that Jessica must have been born the way she was, so even if Marika *had* been a

18

perfect mother Jessica still would have a gender identity problem and a void in her heart where there should have been a core of self-worth. In these respects she was like Julia, so maybe it was something that ran in the family. But if it was, then where had it come from? Her mother's side or her father's side? In pursuing these questions she began to examine the past of her family based on what her mother and her father had told her. She couldn't go deep into the past because she knew almost nothing about her family beyond her parents, who were refugees from the war in Europe. She knew their history because she had listened attentively when they talked about what had happened to them.

Her mother, Bozena, immigrated from Poland in 1946 to escape from the Russians, who had invaded to drive out the Germans but quickly took over and turned Poland into a colony of the Soviet Union. She had lost her family in the war. Her father and her brother were killed resisting the Nazis, and her sister was raped and killed by Russian soldiers. Her mother had died a few years earlier from an untreated heart condition, so at the age of twenty she was living with a grandmother who convinced her she didn't have a future in Poland and connected her with an uncle and aunt who had gone to America before the war and settled in Yonkers. The uncle, Władysław, had a job at Otis Elevator, and the aunt, Anna, had a job at the New York Central Railroad. They owned a building on Nodine Hill, an urban neighborhood populated mostly by immigrants from Poland and Italy. The building had six apartments on three floors, and they lived in one of the apartments, which had two bedrooms. Having no children, they had room for Bozena, so with their sponsorship she came to America as a refugee and moved into their apartment. Since she didn't speak a word of English her job opportunities were very limited, but Ciocia Anna got her a job as a cleaning woman with the Church of St. Casimir, which served the Polish Community. It was a large church with a large rectory, so it was a demanding job keeping everything clean and orderly enough to satisfy the pastor, and it didn't pay well, but at least she had a free place to live, so she was even able to save a little money.

Bozena was a pretty, friendly girl, but for a while her social life was limited to events at the church and the nearby Polish Community Center, which occupied a former armory and had large open rooms that were rented out for wedding receptions, anniversaries, and other occasions. It also had a restaurant and a bar, and occasionally she went to the restaurant with her uncle and aunt, but she never went to the bar, which was for men only. At the Polish Center there were regular meetings of community groups, and every Saturday there was a dance with recorded music. Bozena rarely missed a dance, where she could meet people her age who understood Polish. In fact, the dances were a high point of her life. The other high point was going to Mass, which she did every weekday before starting work and on Sunday with her uncle and aunt. When she was in church she always said a prayer for the souls of her mother, her father, her sister, and her brother, and she thanked God for bringing her to America.

Over the next two years she met a lot of young men at the dances, and she enjoyed dancing with them and in some cases talking with them, but she never went out with any of them. Though she liked most of them, she couldn't imagine being in love with any of them, and she was happy being young and single. She took pride in her job, she had a good relationship with her uncle and aunt, and she was determinedly learning English.

One night at the Polish Center, as she was sitting with a girlfriend while other people danced, a man approached her, a tall man who was very attractive. He stopped in front of her and with a slight bow asked in formal Polish: "Could I have the honor of this dance?"

"You could," she said, rising from her chair.

They were playing a slow piece, a foxtrot, and he gracefully led her into it. That was the first thing she learned about him: he knew how to dance. Since he was holding her at a respectful distance she could surreptitiously glance at his face. He had prominent cheekbones and a regal nose, and he looked like he was several years older than her. And though he held her lightly she could tell he was strong. Continuing to speak in Polish, she said: "My name is Bozena. What's yours?"

"Krysztof," he said, turning his face slightly toward hers but not enough to meet her eyes.

"I haven't seen you here before. Do you live in Yonkers?'

"Yes, I live on Saw Mill River Road."

"Have you lived here long?"

"No, only a month."

"So where did you come from?"

"I came from Poland."

"Where in Poland?"

"Gdańsk," he told her. "Or that's where I'm originally from. I didn't come directly from there. I came from a village in the mountains."

She knew that Gdańsk was on the Baltic, and she knew that the mountains were in the south, but she had never been to either. She had grown up on a farm west of Warsaw and had never travelled until she left Poland to come to America. "What were you doing in the mountains?"

"Escaping from the Russians."

She understood, having heard an unvoiced expletive before the last word. "Do you have family here in Yonkers?"

"Yes. My uncle and aunt with their two children."

"What's their last name?"

"Janczewski," he said.

"Which side of the family is your uncle on, your father's or your mother's?"

"My father's side." He turned his head so that they were facing each other, and with a smile he said: "That's a roundabout way of finding out my last name."

She smiled back. "Well, I couldn't ask you directly."

"Why couldn't you?

"It would have been forward."

"Well, you asked me my first name."

"I know, but that was different."

He gazed at her as if he was trying to figure out how it was different. He had blue eyes, straightforward and honest.

The slow number had ended, and now they were playing a lively polka.

"Would you like to continue dancing?" he asked her.

"Yes, I would." She loved dancing the polka.

He led her with energy around the floor, dancing so well that people stopped to watch them, and she felt as if she had always danced the polka with him.

When the music ended they went to a table, and when he asked her if she wanted a drink she said: "Yes, please. They only have punch."

He brought two plastic cups of punch and sat down with her. After sipping his drink he said: "It's not bad, but it would be better with a spike of vodka."

"That's what my Uncle Władysław says. He sometimes brings his own vodka."

"Good idea. Is he here tonight?"

"No, he and my aunt had another engagement."

"Do you live with them?" he asked after a moment.

"Yeah. How did you guess?"

"You didn't mention your parents."

She took a deep breath before saying: "My father was killed resisting the Nazis, and so was my brother. My sister was raped and killed by the Russians."

"What about your mother?"

"My mother died from an untreated heart condition before I came here."

"So you came here as an orphan?"

"Yes, but I have my uncle and aunt here, and they're wonderful. So I feel lucky. A lot of people don't have anyone."

He nodded in agreement. "My father was killed resisting the Nazis, and my mother was killed resisting the Russians. So I'm basically in the same position as you. And like you I live with an uncle and aunt."

"You said you live on Saw Mill River Road," she said, trying to think who his uncle and aunt were. The name Janczewski was familiar.

"They live above a Polish deli, which they own."

"Oh, yeah. I know the place. We buy kielbasa there."

"If you haven't bought their ham, you should try it. They smoke it themselves."

"We only have ham on Easter, and I don't know where my uncle gets it."

"What's your uncle's last name?"

"Kowalczyk."

"Which side of the family is your uncle on," he asked with a gentle mimicking of her words, "your father's or your mother's?"

"My father's side," she said, appreciating his sense of humor.

"Bozena Kowalczyk, I'm glad to meet you."

"Krysztof Janczewski, I'm glad to meet you. Would you like to dance some more?"

"Aren't you being forward," he asked with smile, "asking me to dance?"

"Well, this dance is lady's choice, though being new here you wouldn't know that. So I'm not being forward at all."

"That's good," he said. "I couldn't handle a forward girl."

They danced and talked until the evening ended, and then he walked her home, even though it was out of his way. With a slight bow he said goodnight and added that he hoped to see her again.

For the next three months they met at dances at the Polish Center, and then he asked her if she would like to go to a movie with him on Sunday afternoon, and she said yes. Of course she had to tell her uncle and aunt who she was going out with, and they both knew his family because her uncle bought Polish food from his uncle, including ham, and her aunt was on the altar society of St. Casimir with his aunt, so they welcomed him when he came to pick her up for their date. By then she knew a lot more about him from their conversations at the dances. Since his English was minimal, he worked at the carpet factory on Nepperhan Avenue, along with hundreds of other recent immigrants, in a job that didn't require much English, but he was taking lessons in the evening at the YMCA in order to improve his English so he could get a better job. Back in Gdańsk he had worked for his father's company which provided maintenance and repair services for ship engines, so he was a highly trained mechanic, and he planned to apply for a job with Otis Elevator by the end of the year when his English would be better. In the meantime he was thankful for his job at the carpet factory.

They walked to the RKO Theater, which was on South Broadway near St. Mary's, and he bought tickets. The movie they were going to see was *High Noon*, which she had heard about from girlfriends at the Polish Center, and she looked forward to seeing Grace Kelly on the screen. She had gone to a few movies with her uncle and aunt, including *Singin' in the Rain*, which they all had enjoyed, but she hadn't gone to many movies because of the language barrier. Since her English had been steadily improving she believed she would be able to understand this movie, but she worried that Krysztof would have trouble understanding it. Luckily, it was an action movie, so she only had to explain a few things to him, especially about the relationship between the characters played by Gary Cooper and Grace Kelly. As they strolled back to Oak Street he suggested that they go to movies regularly because it would help improve his English. He watched television for that purpose, but he preferred going to movies. She wondered if a major reason why he preferred going to movies was being in her company.

After they had gone to the movies several times Krysztof invited her to have Sunday dinner with his family. She joined them after church, and they crowded into his uncle's car, with his uncle and aunt in the front seat and Bozena, Krysztof, and two boys in the back seat, and they drove to Saw Mill River Road. His uncle maneuvered the car into a parking space behind a building, which they walked around and entered through a door into a hall with a staircase leading up to the second floor. Their apartment was spacious, with a large living room and dining room and probably three bedrooms.

The dinner was ready, it only had to be heated up, so his aunt urged them to sit down at the dining room table, which had small bowls of mustard, horseradish, and pickled beets on it. The boys brought serving dishes of kielbasa, pierogi, and kapusta while their father carried a platter with a ham on it. Their mother produced a bottle of sparkling wine, which she poured into glasses around the table. Then she sat down at the foot of the table, opposite her husband, and bowed her head and said grace, followed by the sign of the cross.

"*Na zdrowie!*" the father said, raising his glass.

While he carved the ham they passed the kielbasa, pierogi, and kapusta around the table. Sitting next to him Bozena noticed that he meticulously sliced the ham thin, the way her uncle did, and that made her feel even more at home.

The food was delicious, and after cleaning her plate Bozena complimented them, saying: "That was really good. Do you make everything yourselves?"

"Yes, we make everything except babka and chrusciki," the mother said.

"We used to make them," the father said, "but it's easier to get them from Brooklyn."

"I think your babka was better," the older boy said to his mother.

"Thank you," she told him. "I'll make it myself for your next birthday."

"My birthday comes first," the younger boy said. "Will you make babka for me?"

"Of course. And I'll make it for Bozena too."

"Oh, you don't have to," she protested.

"I'll slice some ham for your uncle and aunt," the father said, "and you can take it with you."

"*Bardzo dziękuję*," she said.

"I understand you clean the church," the mother said after a silence.

"Yes, but I hope to get a better job when my English is better."

"You'll get one, but in the meantime you're doing a wonderful job. I've never seen the church so clean."

"*Dziękuję.*"

"I've known your aunt for many years, and I always felt bad that she couldn't have children. But now I believe that God was saving her for you, and from everything she's told me your coming here was a blessing for her."

"It was also a blessing for me," Krysztof said, gazing across the table at her.

"God's blessing for both of you," the father said, raising his glass of sparkling wine.

A month later she reciprocated by inviting Krysztof to have Sunday dinner with her uncle and aunt. They walked from the church, talking on the way. Her uncle asked Krysztof about his work in Gdańsk doing maintenance and repairs for ship engines, and Krysztof explained in detail what he had done. Her uncle was an expert mechanic, so he understood and appreciated what Krysztof told him. They kept talking even as they climbed the stairs to the apartment. And they stayed in the living room, talking, while Bozena and her aunt went into the kitchen. The roast beef was already cooked and resting on the counter, so all they had to do was prepare the gravy, mash the potatoes, and warm the green beans. As Bozena mashed the potatoes her aunt said: "He seems like a very nice young man."

"He is," Bozena said, valuing her aunt's opinion. She hadn't doubted that her aunt would have a good opinion of Krysztof, but she was glad to hear it.

"He gets along well with your uncle."

"Yeah. They have a common interest in machines."

"Well, maybe your uncle can help him get a job at Otis. I mean, it's good that he has a job at the carpet factory, but he can do better."

She knew that both her uncle and aunt had worked at the carpet factory after their arrival, not knowing a word of English, and if her aunt hadn't gotten her the job at the church she probably would have been working there too. "He knows a lot about machines, though I really can't judge because I know nothing about machines."

After a silence her aunt asked: "Are the uncle and aunt his only family?"

"As far as I know. His sister might be still alive, but he doesn't know what happened to her. His mother was killed trying to stop the Russians from taking her away."

"*Rosjanie to barbarzyńcy*," her aunt said. "Thank God we got out of there before the war."

"Thank God my grandmother got me out of there."

When they left the kitchen they found her uncle and Krysztof in the living room, still talking.

"Come on," her aunt said. "Dinner is ready."

Bozena helped her aunt bring the potatoes, gravy, and green beans while her uncle brought the roast on a platter. They sat down, her aunt said grace, and then her uncle asked Krysztof: "How do you like your roast beef?"

"Well done, please."

"Now, there's a man after my own heart," her uncle said, sharpening his knife. "Bozena likes it medium, and her aunt likes it rare."

"Medium rare," her aunt corrected him.

When he had carved thin slices from the end of the roast and arranged them on a plate, he cut some meat for himself and by then he had reached the part where it was medium. In the meantime, the first plate had been passed to Krysztof, followed by the serving dishes of potatoes and beans, and finally the boat of gravy.

While they were eating, her uncle said: "Krysztof knows a lot about machines. He should work for Otis."

"Then help him get a job there," her aunt said.

"I'll do my best. We could use a good man like him."

It took a few weeks for Krysztof to get an interview with Otis, and though it went well the manager told him to come back in six months, and if by then his English was better he would have a job.

So with that incentive Krysztof started taking lessons five times a week, and six months later he had a job with Otis Elevator.

Since he was now in a much better financial position he proposed marriage to Bozena, she accepted, and then he formally got approval from her uncle and aunt, who paid for the wedding and the reception. Bozena and Krysztof were married in June at St. Casimir, and they had the reception at the Polish Center in a large upper room that accommodated more than one hundred people, mostly from the community. Her uncle had insisted on having a live band, which played a wide range of music from popular to polkas, and for their special dance Bozena and Krysztof selected the polka that they had danced the night they met.

When Marika was born her parents were living in the building owned by her mother's uncle and aunt. Their apartment had two bedrooms, with the possibility of adding a third bedroom if they gave up the living room. Marika had a room all to herself for almost six years, until her sister Julia moved in with her after sleeping in their parents' room for three years. Julia had noisily resisted leaving their parents' room, and Marika wasn't happy to lose the benefits of having her own room, but with each of them in her own twin bed, separated by five feet of neutral territory, they were able to coexist in the room most of the time. When a conflict arose it was usually over Julia's being so messy. At the age of three she had limited potential to mess up the room, other than by throwing her stuffed animals onto the floor, but as she got older she had greater potential, which she fulfilled by littering the floor with wrappers, tissues, and dirty clothes. Marika, who dutifully put her used paper items into a wastebasket and her dirty clothes into a laundry bag, got tired of asking Julia to pick up her things and finally resorted to cleaning up the room herself, which only enabled her sister to become even messier. At one point she asked her mother if they would give up the living room so that she could have her own room again, but instead her mother told Julia to do her part in keeping the room neat and clean, and Julia did change her behavior—for about a week.

There were other differences between the sisters. Marika had inherited features from the northern side of the family: the blond hair, the big blue eyes, the prominent cheekbones, and the rosy complexion along with the sturdy body type, whereas Julia had inherited features from the southern side of the family: the brown hair, the hazel eyes, the long face, and the sallow complexion along with a rangy body type. In fact, Julia didn't look like either her father or her mother, who said that she looked somewhat like the grandmother who had urged her to get out of Poland. In any case, Marika and Julia looked so different that no one would have ever guessed they were sisters.

They were also different in their social behavior. Marika played with girls from the neighborhood and the school. They usually played indoors at each other's homes, and they mainly occupied themselves with dolls and board games. In contrast, Julia played with boys from the neighborhood and the school. They usually played outdoors on the streets, and they mainly occupied themselves with toy guns and war games. Since their father had refused to buy Julia a toy gun, Marika wondered where she had gotten one. Had a boy given it to her? Had she lifted it from the dime store? Their parents didn't know about it, and not being a rat, Marika didn't tell them about it. Julia hid it in the bottom drawer of the bureau they shared, and Marika respected her secret, though she didn't like it that her sister played with guns.

As they got older Marika fell in love with reading, and Julia fell in love with sports. On most Saturday afternoons while Marika went to the library to find books, Julia went to Tibbets Park to play baseball. There were no organized sports at the school, and Julia didn't like basketball, so she wouldn't have played on the church's CYO team if they had allowed girls on it. Instead, she played pickup games of baseball in the park, and apparently she was good enough so that the boys allowed her to play with them.

They both went to St. Casimir School, which went from kindergarten through eighth grade, but with three years between them they rarely saw each other at school, and when they got home Marika hung out with her mother in the kitchen while Julia followed her father around at his maintenance and repair tasks, which after getting home from work he did in reciprocity for a free apartment. From comments that Marika wasn't supposed to hear, her father was uncomfortable having Julia there when he was fixing a toilet that wouldn't flush because someone had dropped a sanitary napkin into it or unplugging a shower drain that was clogged with hair. He didn't think it was proper for a girl to accompany him on such tasks.

After completing eighth grade Marika went to Maria Regina, a Catholic high school for girls in Hartsdale. She got there by bus, which took about forty-five minutes, but there were other girls on the bus going to school with her, so she had company, and she made some new friends. Despite the commute she liked being in a school with only girls because boys were mostly drippy at her age, or else they were a distraction, so it was better not having them around. Since she took to heart what her parents had said about the importance of education, and since she was aware of the sacrifices they were making to send her to a private school, she applied herself to her studies. She was assigned to a section with students whom the nuns expected more of, and though she wasn't the top student she was in the top ten percent. It especially helped that she liked reading, and she got A's in every course except math, which at times she had trouble understanding. At her mother's suggestion she asked her father to help her with algebra, and since he had gone to an excellent high school in Gdańsk he knew the subject and was good at teaching her.

Meanwhile her sister, who was twelve at the time, was still hanging out with boys but she also had a girlfriend who like her was a tomboy. In their mother's opinion the girl, whose name was Audrey, was a bad influence on Julia. One evening, when Julia was late for dinner, their mother smelled smoke on her breath. While questioning her their mother learned that Julia had gotten the cigarette from Audrey. Their mother delivered a stern lecture on the evils of smoking and made Julia promise not to smoke. A few weeks later the school called asking why Julia was absent. Julia had pretended to go to school but instead had played hooky with

Audrey. Again, Julia got a lecture, followed by a reminder of the sacrifices that her parents were making to send her to a private school.

A month later Julia didn't come home for dinner. Marika listened while her mother called information and got the phone number of Audrey's parents and talked with Audrey's mother, who thought her daughter was having dinner with Julia's family. So the girls weren't at either of their homes, and by now it was almost seven in the evening. Marika heard her parents discussing what to do, and her father was about to call the police when the phone rang. Her father answered, and Marika could tell from the expression on his face that he was upset and then angered by what he was being told over the phone. When he finally hung up he reported that it was the police, who had found Julia and another girl at the train station in Tarrytown. The two girls had sneaked onto a train to see how far they could go without tickets, and they had been kicked off at Tarrytown. This time Julia got more than a lecture, she was grounded until further notice, which meant that she had to come home directly after school unless she was involved in a supervised activity. And she was forbidden to play with Audrey.

That night, as they were lying awake in their twin beds, Marika told her sister: "Mom and Dad were worried about you."

"They shouldn't have been worried," Julia said. "I wasn't in danger."

"But they didn't know you weren't in danger, and when a child is missing, parents always imagine the worst."

"How would you know? You're not a parent."

"I know because I know our parents."

"You mean I don't know them?"

"I didn't mean that. I only meant that I know them, and I know they were worried about you."

"And I *wasn't* missing," Julia argued. "I knew where I was."

"But our parents didn't know where you were."

"They didn't have to know where I was."

"As your parents they did. So I hope you don't do that to them again."

Julia was silent, and then she said: "I don't believe they were worried about me because they really don't care about me."

"How can you say that? Mom and Dad love you."

"They don't love me. If I was what they wanted they *would* love me, but I'm not what they wanted so they don't love me."

"What do you think they wanted?"

"Mom wanted another girl like you, and Dad wanted a boy."

"Oh, that's crazy. You *are* what they wanted. Of course when you do things like you did today it makes them unhappy, but it doesn't affect how they feel about you."

"I don't believe that."

Wanting to convince her sister, Marika said: "Do you think God doesn't love you because of what you did today?"

"God has nothing to do with it."

"Yeah, he does. He loves you no matter what you do, and so do Mom and Dad."

Julia was silent again, and then she finally blurted out: "I wish I was a boy."

"You do? Why would you want to be a boy?"

"Because boys can do whatever they want and get away with it. Girls can't get away with anything."

"Well, I wouldn't want to be a boy."

"I know you wouldn't," Julia said. "You're a perfect girl."

"I'm not perfect, but I *am* a girl, and I'm glad I am."

"Yeah, lucky you. But what about me? I have to live with not being a boy."

"I'm sorry," Marika said, meaning it. "But when you get older I think you'll feel different about being a girl."

"Maybe I will," Julia said, "but I don't see how."

After they stopped talking Marika lay on her back for a while and prayed that her sister would believe their parents loved her as she was, which inevitably raised in her mind the question of whether she loved her sister as she was. She hoped she did, but not being sure she ended up praying she did.

THREE

SITTING ON THE deck with the sun now above the trees that sheltered their backyard, Marika hoped her daughter had the resilience to recover from the latest setback. Jessica had recovered from previous setbacks, but this one seemed like the worst so far, and as of now it wasn't certain that she would even recover physically, let alone mentally.

"How are you doing?" Frank asked, coming onto the deck.

"I'm doing okay," she said, facing him. "I was thinking about Jessica. I mean about why she's the way she is."

"Have you concluded anything?"

"No, I haven't."

"Are you sure she wasn't born that way?"

"No, I'm not. But maybe she wasn't born that way."

He put an arm around her shoulder, saying: "You think we did something to make her that way?"

"I think we could have, but I don't know what."

"As her parents we obviously had a major influence on her. But I don't think we did anything to make her that way. If we did, then why isn't Nina that way?"

"Because we treated them differently."

"If we did, then it was because they were different from the day they were born."

Marika considered. "Okay. But if Jessica was born that way, did we accept her as she was?"

"I think we did. We didn't accept her aggressive behavior, but we accepted everything else."

"Well, even if we did, I wonder if we did enough to help her manage her anger."

"I don't know," Frank admitted. "But right now we need to deal with the present situation."

"Yeah, I know."

33

"So let's go get her car."

She had forgotten about the car, which had been left at the address where the EMS picked up Jessica. "Okay. They won't let us see her until later."

Since Jessica frequently mislaid her keys they kept a spare set for her in a drawer of the bureau in their bedroom, so Marika got up and went through the kitchen, leaving her empty mug and plate on the counter next to the sink, and she went upstairs and after some rummaging found the keys.

They went in Frank's car up Roberts Avenue and down to Saw Mill River Road, where they headed south. The address was in a neighborhood where an aunt had lived before it was blighted. The block where they found Jessica's car had suffered from a fire not long ago, and two of the charred houses were abandoned. Luckily the car hadn't been stolen or stripped of parts, so Marika was able to start it and drive it away. She followed Frank back to their house, where she left the car in their driveway, and then she got into his car, and they went to the hospital. By then it was nine-thirty, and visitors would be allowed.

They arrived at Jessica's room just as the doctor had finished making his round. He stopped and talked with them in the hall. He told them that Jessica was stable, and though she was still in a coma the prognosis was good. He didn't commit himself to a time when she might come out of the coma.

Accompanied by the nurse, they went into the room and stood by the bed. Having checked on Jessica during the night so many times over the years, Marika knew she was a restless sleeper, but she looked peaceful now.

"What do you think?" Marika asked the nurse, not completely trusting the doctor.

"I think she's doing well," the nurse said.

"Have you seen a lot of cases like this?"

"Oh, yeah. And I've seen a lot of recoveries."

Marika felt that the nurse wasn't just saying this to make her feel good, and she appreciated it. In fact, it meant more than anything the doctor had said.

They lingered for about an hour, and then after kissing Jessica they left the room and walked to the elevator.

"I need to go to the office," Frank said, "but I can drop you off at home."

"You don't have to," Marika said. "I feel like walking."

"Okay. I'll get home around three so we can come back here."

At that moment the elevator arrived, filled with people who got out as if they didn't know where they were.

They parted with a hug at the entrance of the hospital, and Marika walked to Broadway. If she turned left it would take her to the college, but she had no reason to go there because this summer there was nothing for her to do at the college. Before covid she had spent the summers working at the college's immigrant center, mainly teaching English as a second language and helping people in other ways. But the center still hadn't reopened, so she had a lot of time on her hands. She had managed to get through the previous summer by writing scholarly articles, and though that work had filled the time it hadn't given her the satisfaction she got from working at the immigrant center.

Turning right, she headed up the hill toward Roberts Avenue, thinking about the time when her family was still living on Nodine Hill. She was completing her junior year at Maria Regina, and Julia was graduating from St. Casimir. Their parents were planning to send Julia to Maria Regina, but she didn't want to go there, she wanted to go to Gorton High School, where the boys she hung out with were going. There were long arguments over this issue, but their parents finally refused to let Julia go to Gorton, believing that if she went to Maria Regina she would not only get a better education but also would be separated from the bad influences that got her into trouble. So Julia went to Maria Regina and rode the bus to school with Marika.

Marika was then in her senior year at a school that prepared its students for college, and though neither of her parents had gone to college they both expected her to go to college, so she applied to three colleges that met their criteria of being Catholic and being within commuting distance from home: Fordham, St. Catherine, and Mount Saint Vincent. They all accepted her, and they were all good colleges, but after twelve years of school with only girls Marika wanted to go to a college with boys as well, and that led her to rule out Mount Saint Vincent, which was only for girls. St. Catherine had the advantage of being closer to her home, but it was traditionally a college for girls and had only recently admitted boys, so girls there greatly outnumbered boys, whereas Fordham was traditionally a college for boys and had only recently admitted girls, so boys there greatly outnumbered girls. Though the counselor at Maria Regina, a nun, considered the boy-girl ratio a frivolous reason for selecting a college, Marika felt it was a valid concern, and though Fordham's tuition was higher than St. Catherine's, it offered a bigger scholarship, which offset the financial difference. So in the end it wasn't hard for Marika to convince her parents that Fordham was the place for her.

During the spring of that year her mother's uncle and aunt decided to sell their building. Their main reasons were a desire to simplify their lives and to get out of a neighborhood that had started to decline. They got a good price for the building, and they gave a generous portion of the money to Marika's mother for a down payment on a house. By then her mother had a job at the phone company in customer service, and her father still had a job at Otis Elevator, giving them enough income to pay a mortgage and other expenses of owning a house. They flirted with the idea of leaving Yonkers and buying a house in Hastings, which had a Polish church, but after comparing house prices they decided to stay in Yonkers, and they bought a house in the northwest area of the city on Chase Avenue, a few blocks east of North Broadway. The house, though it was fifty years old, was fifty years newer than the building where they had been living, and its main appeal for Marika's father was that it would need a lot less maintenance. Its main appeal for Marika was that it had three bedrooms, so after all those years of sharing a room with her sister she could finally have a room of her own. And its main appeal for her mother was that her uncle and aunt rented an apartment on North Broadway near Shonnard Place, so they were nearby.

They were settled at their new location when Marika started going to classes at Fordham. Her family had only one car, and since she hadn't expected her father to buy another car for her to drive to Fordham, she had already worked out a bus route to get there. She actually ended up spending no more time on the bus than she had spent commuting to Maria Regina, and during her first week of classes she met a guy who boarded the bus in Riverdale who was also going to Fordham and also majoring in English. He was very entertaining, and he made her laugh with his sardonic comments on famous people and current events. He aspired to be a standup comedian, and he was going to college because his parents wanted him to, which she would learn was the reason most kids went to college.

She had been in class with boys at St. Casimir, but being in class with boys at college was a whole different experience, and she was socially confident enough to thrive in this environment. She hung out in mixed groups, especially in the cafeteria, and she made friends that included both girls and boys. Though she liked the boys and was attracted by some of them, she didn't go beyond being friends with any of them because she was at college to get an education, not to find a husband as some other girls were doing. Also, with her homework and her job at the office of the history department, she didn't have time for a romantic relationship.

By her junior year she had three main girlfriends. One, who was Italian, lived in Manhattan. Another, who was Polish, lived in Brooklyn. And the other, who was Irish, lived in the Bronx. They were all commuters, and they were all English majors. They were often in the same classes, and they hung out together in the cafeteria, welcoming boys who wanted to join them but maintaining their integrity as a group. In the spring semester they decided to take a film course together, thinking it would be easy but it turned out to be hard, with a lot of work. The course met on Friday afternoons, a time when no one wanted to take classes, and afterward they all went into Manhattan together, taking the D train. They usually hung out in Greenwich Village, going to bars and clubs and eating at cheap restaurants. If they were out late,

Marika and the girl from the Bronx would spend the night at the house of the girl from Brooklyn, which had a finished basement where they could crash for the night. The girl's mother, a nice woman, would make breakfast for them in the morning. By senior year the girl from Manhattan and the girl from the Bronx had serious boyfriends, and they got married shortly after graduation. The girl from Brooklyn got married a year later. But they all lived in the New York area, so they continued to see each other.

After graduating Marika got a job with an advertising agency whose office was in midtown, and she began commuting to work. Since she had majored in English they put her on a team of writers, and while she enjoyed working with them she didn't believe that what she was doing had any social value. After all, the purpose of advertising was to get people to buy things they didn't need, and that went against the core values that had been planted in her by her family, her church, and her education.

While she was working for the advertising agency a cardinal from Poland, Karol Józef Wojtyła, was elected Pope, and there was celebration in the Polish community. Within a few weeks her mother had a picture of him hanging on the wall of their living room. Her father was excited because it was believed that the Pope supported the labor movement that had sprung up at a shipyard in Gdańsk, and he avidly began to follow the conflict between the movement and the Soviet government, which became a main topic at the dinner table.

During this time Marika had been looking for a job that matched her values, and the next spring she got a job as an editorial assistant with a small publishing company that was still owned by the family who founded it. The job paid less than her job with the advertising agency, and she started as a glorified secretary, but at least she believed in what she was doing, and it wasn't long before she actually got to do some editing.

In the summer of her second year at the publishing company the Pope made a visit to Poland where according to her father he gave his blessing to the growing demands for independence from Russia. And learning that the Pope was scheduled to visit New

York in early October, her parents got tickets for the Mass in Yankee stadium. When they returned with souvenirs of their experience, as excited as people of her generation returning from a rock concert, Marika was so happy for them.

In the meantime Julia had followed her to Fordham, where she was now a junior majoring in math and taking classes in which she was the only girl. They both still lived at home, but they each had their own bedroom, so they got along better. Their mother still had to scold Julia for being so messy, but since no one else had any reason for being in that room their mother didn't waste much energy trying to get her to clean it up.

Marika had been working at the publishing company for almost two years when she met a guy who sidled up next to her in a bar, asking: "Is this seat free?"

"Yeah," she said, barely looking at him. She had come there with a colleague from work who had left a few minutes ago, and she was about to leave when the guy appeared. She had just taken a larger than usual sip of wine with the intention of finishing it so she could ask for the check and pay.

"Is the food here any good?" the guy asked.

"They have good burgers," she said, taking a better look at him. The guy had an attractive face with fine features and a luscious mouth. And when he turned to look at her she was overwhelmed by his dreamy eyes.

"So maybe I'll have one." He signaled to the bartender, a guy from Ireland, who made single girls feel comfortable at the bar. Without even raising his voice he expelled any guy who got out of line, and though he wasn't big, he somehow gave the impression that it would be dangerous to mess with him.

The guy next to her ordered a draft beer and a hamburger, medium well, with lettuce and tomato and mayonnaise.

Still feeling the effect of his eyes, she said: "You haven't been here before?"

"No. I usually go to places in my neighborhood. But I was

walking by this place on my way to the subway, and I'm hungry, so I thought I'd try it."

She noticed that he didn't have a New York accent, but she didn't know enough about accents to guess where he was from. "Do you live in the city?"

"Yeah, I live on the Upper East Side. I was seeing my aunt," he explained, "who invited me for tea, and all we had to eat were those little watercress sandwiches of white bread with the crusts cut off. You know what I mean?"

She didn't know, not ever having seen such sandwiches. She took a small sip of wine, and just to continue the conversation she asked: "Where does your aunt live?"

"She lives on Beekman Place, not far from here."

"Do you often have tea with her?"

"Too often," he said. "I mean, she's a nice woman, but she's my father's sister, and she's always trying to get me to go back and work for him."

"What does your father do?"

"He manages money."

"And you don't like managing money?"

"I don't like doing things for rich people. I'd rather do things for poor people."

That was appealing. He wasn't like most of the guys she had met in the city whose only goal was to make money. "So are you doing things for poor people?"

"Well, they're not exactly poor," he said, "but they're underserved by our society."

"Who are you talking about?"

"My students at Hunter College."

"You teach at Hunter?"

"Yeah, I'm an instructor there."

"What do you teach?"

"English literature."

"That's great. Do you like teaching?"

"I love it," he said with passion. "I'm working on a doctorate there so I can get a full-time position."

Impressed, she asked: "How long will it take you to get your doctorate?"

"If all goes well, I can probably get it in another three years."

"That's not too long. What do you have to do to get it?"

"I have to write a dissertation."

"What about?"

He cocked his head. "Do you really want to know?"

"Yeah, or I wouldn't have asked."

"The short stories of John Cheever."

"Really? I love those stories." She had read several of them in a course on modern American literature. She remembered her professor saying they weren't supposed to be in the course because the author was still alive, so please don't tell anyone.

"Were you an English major?" he asked her, looking at her doubtfully.

"Don't I look like one?"

"No, you don't."

"So what do English majors look like?"

"I don't know, but they don't look like you."

"What do I look like?"

Gazing at her tenderly, the guy said: "You look like someone from another country."

Of course she was aware of her Slavic features, and more than once people had stopped her on the street and asked her if she spoke English. But what this guy had just told her sounded like a genuine compliment. "Well, I really was an English major."

"Where did you go to college?"

"Fordham."

"That's a great university," he said, "and they have a great English program."

"Where did you go?"

"I went to Princeton," he said modestly.

She had heard of Princeton, but she had never known anyone who went there. Putting that together with his accent and his aunt who lived on Beekman Place, she concluded that he must come from a rich family. "What's your name?"

"Thayer," he said.

"And where did you grow up?"

"Darien, Connecticut."

That clinched it: he was a WASP. "Well, my name is Marika. It's a Polish name. And I grew up in Yonkers."

"That's interesting," he said as if it was. "Where do you work?"

She named the company.

"That's a great company. In fact, we use your anthology of short stories in one of the courses I teach at Hunter."

"I helped to edit the latest edition."

"Then you should autograph my copy of it."

Laughing, she said: "Yeah, that would raise its value."

"It would," he said seriously.

At that point the bartender served the hamburger, which at least for a while got Thayer's undivided attention.

She had told her mother she wouldn't be home in time for dinner, but she couldn't linger because she had to catch a train and then take a bus home from the Yonkers station, so after finishing her wine she asked the bartender for the check.

"You have to go?" Thayer asked, chewing his last bite of food.

"Yeah, I have to catch a train."

"Where do you live?"

"In Yonkers. I still live at home with my family."

He nodded. "Yeah. I know what that's like. You should get an apartment in the city."

"I would," she said, "but I can't afford it. Eventually, yes, but not for a while."

"I understand. Can I see you again?"

"Well—" She wanted to see him again, but she almost always went home directly after work because her family had dinner at a certain time. Tonight was an exception because her colleague had wanted to talk about a problem she was having with her boss. "I could meet you here next week."

"I teach classes on Tuesdays and Thursdays" he said. "Would Wednesday work for you?"

"Yeah, it would," she said, paying the check with a credit card and leaving a tip in cash for the bartender.

"What time?" he asked.

"Oh, I don't know. Around five-thirty?"

"Perfect," he said, gazing at her with those dreamy eyes.

"So I'll see you then," she said, descending from the bar chair.

As she left the bar she could feel his eyes following her as if he wanted to go with her wherever she was going.

They began meeting regularly on Wednesdays. He would get there first, they would have a drink at the bar, and then they would sit in a booth and have dinner. In the relative privacy of the booth they talked, and talked, and talked, and talked, learning more about each other. Since he had never met anyone like her, he wanted to know all about her family, going back to Poland, and it made her feel special. They also talked about his family, about his job at Hunter College, and about his dissertation. Outside of their families the main topic of their conversations was the books they had read and liked. For all their background differences they had a major thing in common: their love of reading.

She always had to leave by nine because she knew her parents would worry if she took a later train, and the buses ran only every hour at that time. Unlike the other guys she had met in bars he made no hint about her going to his apartment, and he never tried to kiss her goodnight, though she wouldn't have minded. What he did after a few months was invite her to attend one of his classes. Since it ended by eight she could catch a subway at Hunter that in three stops would take her to Grand Central, and since she wanted to know what Thayer was like as a teacher, she had a strong motive for accepting his invitation. Also, the course material was the anthology of short stories that she had edited, which gave her an extra reason for attending. So on a Thursday after work she took a subway to 68th Street and met Thayer in front of the main building of the college.

As soon as he led her into the building she felt the buzz of students on their way to class, though it was different from

Fordham, where she had gone to day classes. These students were mostly older, and they probably worked during the day. When she entered Thayer's classroom she noted that the students were mostly African American, Hispanic, and Asian, and they were mostly wearing tee shirts and jeans. Thayer had explained in advance that they weren't English majors, they were taking this course because it was required for undergraduates, which presented challenges. Presumably following the established routine, they had arranged the desks in a U-formation with the instructor's desk at the open end of it.

When it was time for the class to begin, Thayer closed the door and introduced Marika to the students as a friendly observer who had nothing to do with the college so they should relax and pretend she wasn't there. She sat at a desk at one end of the U-formation and tried to make herself invisible, though she was conscious of being the only white, blond woman in the room, which made her an object of curiosity for the students.

From Thayer's description of the course she knew its purpose was to enable students to read critically, write correctly, and speak effectively. And she knew the assignment for today was to read "A Rose for Emily" by William Faulkner, a story she had read over and over for a course at Fordham. The students in Thayer's course were expected to write a one-page paper about what they got out of the story and be prepared to discuss several assigned study questions. Beginning with the student at the end of the formation opposite Marika, the students reported the main ideas from their papers and responded to questions from other students. Marika was impressed by how perceptive and articulate they were, and though there was a range of performance levels from excellent to poor, the average was very good. She was also impressed by Thayer's ability to draw ideas out of students and get them to interact with each other. She thought he was as good as any teacher she had at Fordham, most of whom had been excellent.

This activity was followed by Thayer calling on students and asking them to respond to an assigned study question. He got other students to join a discussion, and then he went to the next student with another study question. He went around the formation randomly, skipping a student and coming back, so they didn't know exactly when they would be called on and would therefore stay attentive. At one point he had about five students involved in a discussion, going back and forth, and even digressing, which he allowed as long as it was productive.

At the end of the class he told them what a good job they had done, and he turned to Marika inviting her to make a comment. Sincerely, she told them: "You were great. I'd love to be in a class with you guys."

When the students had filed out of the classroom Thayer said: "Thanks for attending. And thanks for your comment. They need all the encouragement they can get."

"I meant it," she told him.

"I know," he said.

They left the building, and he walked her to the subway. Pausing at its entrance, she said: "You know what? You've inspired me. I want to get a master's in English. Can you tell me how to get into the program?"

"Yeah. Sure." He gazed at her appreciatively as if she had given him validation for teaching English at Hunter College instead of working for his father. And that led to their first physical interaction—a heartfelt hug.

She started the master's program in September, with classes on Tuesdays and Thursdays that met in the evening at Julia Richmond High School, which was near Hunter. The classes ended at eight fifteen so she could catch a train that arrived in Yonkers at nine thirty, though she couldn't have dinner with her family. Both her parents were glad that she was continuing her education. They were proud of her for being the first in her family to go to college, get a degree, and now pursue another degree. So they did everything they could to accommodate her.

By then her sister Julia had graduated from Fordham with a degree in math and was working on Wall Street as a member of a team that traded bonds and other securities. Julia was the only female on the team, and when she tried to describe to their parents what she did at work she talked just like one of the guys, occasionally slipping with an expletive, which didn't go over well with their parents. She still lived at home, but she wasn't always there for dinner because after work she sometimes hung out with her colleagues.

After a few weeks of classes Marika became friends with a woman in her course on 18th century English literature, whose name was Evelyn. They began to meet in the cafeteria before class to have a coffee and a snack to fortify themselves for the class, and from those meetings Marika learned that Evelyn was from upstate and had a bachelor's in English from Binghamton. She had a good job in the communications department of a large retail company whose head office was on 6th Avenue, at a salary that enabled her to share an apartment in the East 80s with another woman. For almost six years the arrangement had worked well for her, with two successive roommates, but her current roommate planned to get married in early November, so she needed to find another roommate. She had been looking for a roommate but hadn't found one, and after hearing how much time Marika spent each day commuting, she floated the idea of sharing the apartment. They would each have their own bedroom, and they would each pay half of the rent, which was low because the apartment was under rent control. There was only one rule, based on Evelyn's experience with roommates, and that was not to bring any guys back to the apartment.

Marika could see the advantages of living in the city, including not only the time it would save her from commuting but also the time it would give her to hang out later in the evening with Thayer. The only disadvantage she could see was that her parents didn't want her to leave home. So over the next several days she tried to get them to accept the idea, arguing that her roommate was a responsible woman who had a good job and was pursuing a master's at Hunter College, the apartment was in a good neighborhood, she could afford the rent on her salary, she would be living only thirty minutes from Yonkers, and she would come home on Sundays to attend Mass and have dinner with her family.

Reluctantly, they agreed to let her try it, subject to their inspection of the apartment, which Marika understood as a way for them to meet Evelyn and make sure that she was a suitable roommate for their daughter. As it turned out, they both liked Evelyn, and her being Catholic was icing on the cake. They even gave Marika money to buy the departing roommate's furniture, which included a bed, a chest of drawers, and two chairs, so late in November she moved into the apartment, an event that she and Evelyn celebrated with a pizza and a bottle of California champagne. The next day they formalized the arrangement by meeting with the landlord and getting Marika put on the lease, so she could keep the rent control if for any reason Evelyn departed in the future.

FOUR

FOR LUNCH SHE made herself a tuna salad sandwich that she ate out on the deck. When she was done eating she needed to kill time until Frank returned, so she found a novel that she had been planning to read, and back on the deck she sat down and started the novel. But it didn't engage her, and before long her mind returned to the question of what she might have done wrong with Jessica. She retraced her way around a rotary, wondering if she should have gotten off at a different exit, which led her back to the time when she moved into the apartment.

As she got settled she began to enjoy the benefits of living in the city, which included not having to get up so early in the morning because instead of commuting from Yonkers, which took at least an hour door-to-door if all went well, she only had a ten-minute walk to the subway, a ride with three stops to 51st Street, and a five-minute walk to her office. There were also the benefits of not having to cut her evenings short to catch a train to Yonkers, so she could have dinner with Evelyn after their classes, and she could spend more time with Thayer. But she kept her commitment to spend Sundays with her family not only out of a sense of duty but also out of a need to maintain her relationship with them. Her father made it easy for her by picking her up at the Woodlawn subway station and driving her home, so she only had to walk to the station at 86th Street.

On a Sunday in the middle of December the priest at St. Casimir, instead of doing a normal homily, alerted them to the military takeover of Poland and the imposition of martial law to crush the movement that had begun in Gdańsk the previous year and evolved into a labor union. The union was called Solidarność, which meant Solidarity, and its leader was a shipyard worker named

Lech Wałęsa. The union's influence had expanded beyond Gdańsk and become a serious threat to the Russian domination of Poland. In response the Russians installed a military dictator, General Wojciech Jaruzelski, whose job at their command was to repress Solidarity and every other form of resistance. The priest recounted the brutal measures the government was taking, and he led the congregation in a prayer for Poland to gain its independence from Russia. Of course that became a main topic of conversation during Marika's weekend visits to her parents.

Meanwhile, she continued seeing Thayer on Wednesday, but now that she was living in the city she could also see him on Friday or Saturday. She preferred Saturday because like most other people she was tired on Friday after a week of work, but as time passed she began to see him on both Friday and Saturday. Typically, they would meet in a bar and have dinner and linger there for hours, talking and sipping glasses of wine. Sometimes they would go to a movie, usually a foreign film because he didn't like the typical Hollywood films, or to a play, usually off-Broadway because he didn't like the typical Broadway musicals and comedies. And Marika found that she liked what he liked, which reinforced their relationship.

Though he lived only a few blocks away from her she didn't go to his apartment until a snowy Friday night in February. It wasn't planned, it just happened because of the weather. His apartment had one bedroom, and it was furnished simply, with an emphasis on bookshelves, which lined two whole walls of his living room. At one end was a desk, piled with notepads and papers, and next to the sofa was a stereo unit, with stacks of cassettes.

After taking off her coat she followed him into the kitchenette, where he got a bottle of white wine out of the refrigerator. Since he drank red wine she wondered if he had bought it for her in the hope that sooner or later she would come there.

"Thank you," she said, taking a glass of wine from him.

While he poured himself a glass of red wine she headed back into the living room, sat down on the sofa, and took a sip of wine.

Returning from the kitchenette, he asked: "Would you like some music?"

"Yeah, sure," she said. Though her knowledge of music didn't go much beyond the polkas they played at the Polish Center, the jazz her father played on the stereo, and the pop songs they played on the radio, she was open to anything, and when he put on some piano music she really liked it. "What's that?"

"It's Chopin," he told her. "I thought you might like it."

Of course she knew who Chopin was, and she had heard his music at the Polish Center, military pieces that inspired displays of patriotism from people standing at attention. She hadn't known that Chopin composed other kinds of music.

He joined her on the sofa, saying: "Music gives me peace."

"I don't know much about music," she said. "I never took a course in it."

"I never did either," he said. "I learned about it from a guy at college, a graduate student. I heard him playing the piano while I was walking by the building where they had the music program. The sound came out through an open window, and I stopped to listen. It was beautiful, and I stayed to listen until it was done. I don't know why, but for some reason I waited there until a guy came out of the building, and I asked him if he'd been playing the piano. He said yes, and he asked me if I liked it. I said I did, and I asked him who the composer was. He laughed, I mean in a nice way, and he said it was Mozart. Then he asked me if I would like to learn about music, and I said yes. And he said he would teach me about music."

Touched, she said: "I wish I'd met someone like that."

"Yeah, I was lucky. As an undergraduate you didn't mingle with graduate students. They lived on a separate campus."

"So how did he teach you about music?"

"Twice a week in the evening," he said, "I'd go to his room in the graduate college, a building with a gothic tower, and he would play from his collection of records. He started with early choral music and took me through the different periods up to the present. But it wasn't strictly linear, we'd go back and revisit his favorite composers."

"Who were his favorite composers?"

"Bach, Handel, Mozart, Beethoven, Brahms, Chopin, Verdi, and Wagner. At least he played their music the most."

"Who were your favorites?

"Bach and Mozart."

"Did he become a performer?"

"Oh, no. He didn't like performing. He didn't like having audiences."

"He must have liked having you as an audience."

A look of regret filled Thayer's eyes. "No, that wasn't it. He liked me."

"You mean as a friend?" she asked, not understanding.

"As more than a friend. I mean, it turned out that he was gay."

Intrigued, she waited for him to continue.

"But I wasn't gay, and I let him know I wasn't."

"How did you find out he was gay?"

"He asked me to spend the night with him."

"And how did he react when you turned him down?"

"He didn't want to see me again," Thayer said sadly. "He ended the relationship."

She could tell it had hurt him, and wanting to comfort him she said: "At least you learned about music from him."

"Yeah. But I would have liked to continue the relationship. In a way he was the best friend I ever had."

"Did you see him after that?"

"No. I tried to see him, but he was done with me. I wasn't what he wanted."

"Well, we can't always be what other people want."

"I know we can't, but I have the same problem with my father," Thayer said as if it hurt him very deeply. "I mean, I'm not what my father wants."

"What does he want?"

"He wants a son exactly like him."

"But doesn't your father want you to be happy?"

Thayer sighed. "I guess he does. But he can't imagine how I could be happy teaching English at Hunter College."

"That's his problem, not yours. If you're happy doing what you love, then he should be happy that you're happy."

"I guess he should," he said, looking at her appreciatively.

She was well into her third glass of wine when he leaned over and kissed her, and she was aroused by his luscious mouth. After a while they started going beyond kissing, and there were points where she could have stopped it, but he was so considerate, so sensitive to her feelings, that she let herself go. And they ended up spending the night in his bed.

Luckily, the next morning it was Saturday, not Sunday when she would have had to go to Yonkers and attend Mass with her family, but as soon as she woke up she began to worry about being pregnant, and she was conscious of having committed a mortal sin. These two concerns were so intertwined that it was hard to separate them, and lying there in Thayer's bed she was already sorry for what she had done.

At least when she got up to pee she wasn't naked, she was wearing a shirt that Thayer had thoughtfully given her to wear in bed. Of course she was sore, but there wasn't any more blood, so there was no physical evidence of her sin. And she was relieved to see no evidence on her face when she looked at herself in the bathroom mirror.

"Are you all right?" Thayer asked her when she returned to the bedroom.

"Yeah," she said, hiding her concerns.

"I didn't plan for that to happen."

"I didn't either," she said, getting back into bed with him.

He reached over and drew her toward him and gently hugged her, saying: "I didn't know it was your first time."

"Well, it was."

"So you're not on the pill?"

"No. I'm not supposed to be on the pill."

"I understand. But you might want to think about it."

"I hope I'm not already pregnant."

"When was your last period?"

"Two weeks ago."

He sighed. "Well, if you *are* pregnant, then we'll get married."

She liked him, she really liked him, and though she hadn't thought about marrying him, she saw that if she was pregnant it would be the only acceptable course of action because she ruled out having an abortion or being an unwed mother. So it was comforting to have what sounded like a proposal. "I wouldn't want you to marry me because you feel you have to."

"I wouldn't feel I have to, I'd want to."

She thanked him by kissing him on the cheek.

After a while she needed to get up and go home and take a shower. He didn't try to hold her back, and as she was leaving he said: "Don't worry. Everything will be all right."

She understood how he could say that having dealt with her concern about being pregnant, but she hadn't talked about her other concern, which was something he couldn't deal with. It was her concern alone.

Back at her apartment she was greeted by the smell of coffee. Evelyn was always there on Saturday because her boyfriend, who had a job with a beverage distributor, always had to work on Saturday, so she would spend the night at his place on Saturday and Sunday and come home early on Monday morning to change into her clothes for work.

After a brief exchange with Evelyn she went into her bedroom, closed the door, undressed, and put her clothes into the laundry bag. Then, wearing a robe that her mother had given her, she went into the bathroom and took a long shower, wishing she could wash away her sin.

Dressed in clean clothes, she had breakfast with Evelyn, who had bought some pastries from a nearby German bakery. She knew that Evelyn was on the pill because she had seen it in the medicine cabinet, so she broached the subject by saying: "If I decided to go on the pill, how would I get it?"

"You'd need a prescription," Evelyn said. "You could get one from my doctor."

"Well, I haven't decided. I'm only thinking about it."

Evelyn paused to take a sip of coffee and then said: "If you're sleeping with Thayer, you shouldn't just be thinking about it. You should go on the pill right away."

"But we're not supposed to use that kind of birth control."

"I know, and we're not supposed to have sex before we're married. But those rules were made by men who have no idea what it's like being a woman."

"So you don't believe that having sex before you're married is a mortal sin?"

"No, I don't believe that it's any kind of sin. I'm not hurting anyone. In fact, I'm sharing love with someone."

"When you go to confession, do you tell the priest what you've been doing?"

"I don't go to confession anymore."

"Do you take communion?"

"Oh, yeah. I believe that God understands. I mean, he knows all about me, so why wouldn't he understand?"

"If your parents knew, would they understand?"

"No way," Evelyn said. "They still think I'm a virgin, and why should I hurt them by telling them I'm not? When I get married, it won't make any difference."

"I guess it won't."

"But if I got pregnant, my parents would know, and that's why I'm on the pill. I don't want to embarrass them."

"So you're doing it for your parents?"

"Yeah. Of course I'm doing it for myself, but I'm also doing it for my parents."

Marika liked this rationalization. She had never done anything before that would have embarrassed her parents, so she was in uncharted territory, and she was grateful for having some guidance from her more experienced roommate.

As usual on Sunday she took the subway to Woodlawn, where her father was waiting to pick her up and take her home. As usual he asked her about her job, about her courses, about her apartment, and about her roommate. He didn't ask her about Thayer because he didn't know she had an ongoing relationship with the guy who had inspired her to go back to school and get a master's degree. And after what had happened last night she resolved to keep that relationship to herself for the time being.

At home she found her mother in the kitchen, wearing an apron and preparing dinner. As usual she hugged her mother, hoping her mother wouldn't sense anything different about her, and evidently her mother didn't because she didn't ask any questions. Marika hung out in the kitchen until her sister appeared from upstairs, and at least she didn't have to worry about Julia sensing anything different about her because Julia didn't notice things about other people, being completely absorbed in herself. She wasted no time in letting Marika know how much money her team had made in trading that week, and she kept talking in the car while their father drove them to church.

Except for special holidays they no longer attended St. Casimir because there was a parish in the neighborhood, close enough to walk to in warmer weather. It was called St. Brigid, and since it had a smaller building than St. Casimir and a large active congregation it was packed for the eleven o'clock Mass on Sundays, so they always got there early enough to claim room on their usual pew, which was near the front on the left side, a location that most people avoided because it was directly in the priest's line of vision from the pulpit. Marika previously hadn't minded sitting in this exposed location, but today she felt uncomfortable and wished they were sitting in a back pew over on the right side with people who came late.

During the penitential rite she was conscious of the sin she had committed last night, and she wondered if she should refrain from taking communion. But if she did, her parents would wonder why, and they would be worried, so after a torturous debate with herself she decided to take communion as usual, based on the principle of not worrying her parents.

As usual the conversation at dinner was dominated by Julia, who among other things talked about her intention to move into the city and live in Tribeca, a cool upcoming neighborhood. Their parents expressed concern about it, and they tried to persuade her to live in the kind of neighborhood where Marika lived, but she rejected their advice, arguing that Tribeca was closer to her office. After a discussion their parents agreed to consider the possibility, and Julia agreed not to sign a lease without their approval of the neighborhood and the apartment. Since this discussion occupied most of the time they spent at the dinner table, Marika was glad that her sister monopolized their parents' attention, deflecting it from her and providing cover for what she was hiding.

In the late afternoon their father drove her to the Yonkers station, and when he left her she was relieved that the visit to her family was over. She had never felt that way before, she had always felt a little sad going back to the city. But today she felt different.

Two days later she had an appointment with Evelyn's doctor, who examined her thoroughly before prescribing the pill for her. Evelyn had warned her about the examination, but she was still discomfited by it because her only experience with doctors was with the family doctor, who had given her shots and treated her for occasional skin rashes. But as she left the doctor's office with a prescription in hand, she welcomed the possibility of freedom, though the fear of being pregnant still hung over her.

Marika started taking the pill right away, abetted by the rationalization that she was doing it for her parents, but she didn't have sex with Thayer again until she learned that she wasn't pregnant. Thayer understood, so he refrained from initiating anything, and she appreciated his consideration. She also valued the backup he had given her by promising to marry her if she was pregnant, though she was thankful that she didn't have to go through the process of a rushed marriage to someone she hadn't even told her parents about. And that made her consider telling her parents about him.

Over the next several months their relationship continued with their meeting two or three times a week, hanging out in neighborhood bars, eating at inexpensive restaurants, going to movies and sometimes to plays, and even attending a concert of a famous pianist playing Mozart concertos. The most important change was that she now spent Friday nights at Thayer's apartment and the next morning took a shower there and had breakfast, which he prepared, usually an omelet and bread from a bakery. As spring turned to summer she began to think about the possibility of marrying Thayer, not in a shotgun wedding but in a normal, planned wedding.

By then she had told her parents about him, and at their urging they finally met him. They arranged to meet at the Chart House, a riverside restaurant in Dobbs Ferry where her parents occasionally ate on Saturday nights. It was right next to the train station, so they could take a train there. She wore a summer dress, and Thayer wore the WASP uniform of blue blazer, white button-down shirt, rep tie, and khaki pants. If nothing else, she was confident that Thayer would make a good visual impression.

The dinner went well. Thayer was courteous and respectful to her parents, responding openly to her father's questions about his work and her mother's questions about his family. He shared an interest in sports with her father and an interest in cooking with her mother. They ended the meal with her father buying shots of Polish vodka and toasting Thayer with a hearty: "*Na zdrowie!*"

"Nasdrovia!" Thayer said, echoing him with not a bad accent.

To avoid her having to come back to Yonkers the next morning she and Thayer had agreed that she would spend the night with her parents and he would go back to the city, so they waited until he boarded a train before going home.

On the way her father commented: "Your friend is very well educated."

"And very polite," her mother added.

Later, when her father had gone upstairs her mother stayed in the living room with her. Their conversation began with her mother asking in Polish: "How serious is your relationship with this young man?"

"Serious enough for me to think you should meet him."

"Where did he grow up?"

"In Connecticut."

"Where did he go to college?"

"Princeton."

"So his family must have money," her mother said as if this wasn't necessarily a good thing.

"I believe they do, but he doesn't care about money."

"I can tell he really loves teaching."

"Yeah. And when he completes his doctorate he'll have a full-time job at Hunter."

"He doesn't want to teach at Princeton?"

"No, he wants to teach kids who don't have the advantages of kids who go to Princeton."

"I admire him for that. So he has a mission."

"Yeah, he does."

After a silence her mother asked: "Is he the reason why you decided to go back to school and get a master's degree?"

She nodded. "Yeah. I attended one of his classes, and he was such a good teacher, he inspired me."

"But that was almost a year ago. So why didn't you tell us about him earlier?"

"I don't know. I guess I felt that if I told you about him it would mean I was serious about him, and I really wasn't sure if I was serious about him."

"I understand," her mother said. "As far as I know, you don't have a lot of experience with men."

"I don't. Thayer is the first." After saying this she hoped it only meant to her mother that Thayer was her first boyfriend.

"Well, he seems to have a lot of good qualities, but I hope you don't rush into marrying him."

"Do you have doubts about him?"

"No, I don't. I have doubts about whether you're ready to make a lifetime commitment to a man. It *is* a lifetime commitment, you know."

"Yeah, I know. I've only begun to think about marrying him."

"It's all right to think about it," her mother told her, "but don't make any decision for a while. Take your time."

"I don't have all the time in the world. I'm twenty-seven."

"You still have time to get to know him better before you make any decision."

Lying in bed awake that night she went over this conversation, and she wondered if her mother had detected something in Thayer that made her have doubts about him. Her mother had said she didn't have doubts, but what if she just had a feeling about him?

After resolving to follow her mother's advice on the matter she went to sleep.

During that summer Marika was taking one course in the master's program and Thayer was teaching one undergraduate course, so they were both occupied two evenings a week. They usually met on two or three of the other evenings, and she always spent the night with him on Friday. She really liked being with him, and she could imagine living with him. But on a Saturday morning after her shower she was looking in the medicine cabinet for an aspirin when she spotted a plastic freezer bag of white powder. She had no experience with drugs, but she knew that cocaine was a white powder, and it wasn't likely that the content of the bag was powdered sugar.

Wrapped in a bath towel, she went into the kitchenette where Thayer was stirring a bowl of eggs in preparation for making an omelet. He looked so innocent that she hesitated, but then she said: "There's a bag of white powder in the medicine cabinet. What is it?"

"Oh, it's nothing," he said, avoiding her eyes.

"Is it a drug?"

"Yeah, it's a drug."

"Do you take it?"

"Sometimes, but not every day."

Confused, she asked: "Why do you take it?"

"I take it to get high when I feel low. I also take it before teaching."

"Why do you take it before teaching?"

"To help me perform."

"You mean what I saw you doing in the classroom was a performance?"

"Of course it was," he said, finally facing her. "If I don't entertain my students, they'll lose interest, and they won't learn a thing."

"So you need this drug to enhance your performance?"

"Well, it helps me do a better job."

"But why would you need it? I thought you love teaching."

"I do love teaching."

Deeply concerned about him, she asked: "Could you live without this drug?"

"I don't know," he said with tears forming in his eyes.

"Then you better think about it," she told him. "Because I know I couldn't live *with* it."

Nodding, he murmured: "I'll think about it."

She gave him a hug, and then she went into the bedroom and got dressed. Before leaving she went back into the kitchenette, where he was still standing, staring into the bowl of eggs, and she gave him another hug, saying: "Call me when you know."

"Okay," he said.

She didn't start crying until she had left the building and was walking down the street. She knew that whatever he did about his drug habit she had lost the person who had inspired her. She had lost him because he wasn't what she had thought he was.

Back at the apartment she found Evelyn sitting at the table in their dining area, eating breakfast and reading a book. She almost didn't stop, but Evelyn looked up and said: "You don't look happy."

"I'm not happy."

"Why aren't you happy?"

Not being sure she had handled the situation well, she decided to share her discovery with Evelyn, and she sat down in the chair opposite her, asking: "What would you do if you found out that your boyfriend had a drug habit?"

"I'd dump him," Evelyn told her without hesitation.

"You would? Why?"

"Because the drug would always come first, and I'd come second."

"You wouldn't want to help him break the habit?"

"I'd want to, but I'd know I couldn't."

"How would you know that?"

"I'm not a therapist, and even therapists have trouble getting people to break drug habits." Evelyn paused and then explained: "I have a cousin with a drug habit. His father and mother have spent a lot of money on therapists without success."

"What drug is your cousin taking?"

"Cocaine."

"Is cocaine addictive?"

"Of course it is."

"Well, I have to admit," Marika said, "I never knew anyone with a drug habit. So I don't know anything about it."

"Why are you asking?" Evelyn said. "Did you find out that Thayer has a drug habit?"

"Yeah, I did. This morning I found a bag of white powder in his medicine cabinet."

"That sounds like cocaine, though it could be something else."

"Whatever it is, he takes it to enhance his performance in teaching."

"Oh, my God. That's what rock musicians do."

"He says it helps him do a better job."

"So what did you tell him?"

"I told him he better think about whether he could live without that drug because I knew I couldn't live *with* it."

"You did the right thing. And don't even think about helping him give it up. He needs professional treatment."

"So I should tell him to get treatment?"

"Yeah. But don't hold your breath. It takes a long time for people on drugs to break a habit, and in many cases they never break it."

Confronting what looked like a hopeless situation, Marika started crying again, and Evelyn got up and came around the table to comfort her. With an arm around her shoulder Evelyn said: "I know it hurts. But you'll get over it. You will."

With her heart broken, she didn't see how she would ever get over it.

FIVE

SHE WAS LOST in the past when Frank came out onto the deck. She roused herself and checked her watch and saw it was almost three o'clock. She got up and followed him through the kitchen and out the front door, stopping on the way to go to the bathroom. As they drove to the hospital he told her about the new project he was working on. She was always interested in his work, and she understood that he was talking about it to distract her from the worry about Jessica.

When they got to Jessica's room the doctor was examining her, and they waited in a room at the end of the hall that overlooked the river. Since two other people were in the room they couldn't talk, so they waited in silence to hear from the doctor. While Frank checked messages on his phone Marika gazed out the window at the river, whose surface now was as smooth as glass, and her mind returned to the time when she was living in the city, trying to find her way in life.

In the fall after she broke up with Thayer she took two courses in the master's program, moving along toward her degree. Since her courses were at Julia Richmond and Thayer's courses were in the main building, she didn't run into him at the college. And she didn't hear from him, which of course hurt though the pain was attenuated by the passage of time.

Meanwhile her sister had left home and moved into a loft in Tribeca without a roommate, and when Julia mentioned how much rent she was paying, Marika got the message that her sister was making a lot more money than she was. Of course she didn't care about making money, she was happy to be doing something she loved and something that contributed to society, so she didn't feel put down by the comparison, but she was annoyed by her sister's assumption that money was an appropriate measure of their value. She visited the loft, and she told Julia how cool it was, but she didn't go back there, and though they both lived in the city they only saw each other on the Sundays when Julia visited their parents, which wasn't often.

Marika had started going to Yonkers on Saturday when she had nothing to do that night, as was usually the case now that she was no longer seeing Thayer. She couldn't hang out with Evelyn, who spent Saturday night with her boyfriend, and she didn't want to hang out in a bar alone, waiting for a guy to approach her. She preferred the company of her parents to guys who didn't have a date on Saturday night, so she was at home on the Saturday before Thanksgiving when her mother asked her if she had seen Julia lately.

"No. I haven't," she replied. "We live in different worlds."

Sounding worried, her mother said: "We haven't seen her or heard from her since the last time she was here, and that was more than six weeks ago."

"Well, she'll be here for Thanksgiving."

"I hope so. I wish she'd let us know if she's coming."

"I'll call her and remind her," she said, annoyed with her sister for not communicating with their mother.

When she called and reminded her Julia said she didn't need to be reminded and their parents should know she was coming for the holiday. Marika gently urged her to call their mother and confirm it. And they agreed to meet at Grand Central for a train that would get to Yonkers before noon.

Julia got there at the last minute, and they almost missed their train. They had to run down the ramp to the platform to make it before the doors closed.

On the ride to Yonkers she had to listen to Julia talk about her important role on the team, about the money she was making, and about the trip to Mallorca she was planning. After enduring her sister's self-aggrandizement Marika was relieved when the train finally pulled into the Yonkers station.

Julia started talking as soon as they were in their father's car, and he drove them home without trying to break through the monologue. Uncle Walter and Ciocia Anna were there, seated in the living room drinking Manhattans, which their father made for special occasions. After an exchange of greetings with them Marika went into the kitchen to help her mother while Julia sat down with them and started talking.

By the time they sat down at the dinner table Uncle Walter had taken over the conversation by switching into Polish, which for some reason Julia had never learned, and her mother said grace in Polish before her father began carving the turkey. Not knowing what would happen in the near future they had a good time eating and drinking, and even Julia finally stopped talking about herself and joined in the festivities.

Two Saturdays later when Marika went to Yonkers, without Julia, her father picked her up at the Woodlawn station, and as soon as she got into the car he told her that Otis Elevator was closing its plant in Yonkers. She had heard about the changes after the company was acquired by United Technologies, including the series of layoffs that began three years later, but she was still shocked by the news that they were closing the plant. Her father had worked there for thirty years, and now at the age of fifty-eight he was being laid off.

As they drove out of the parking lot she asked: "Why are they closing the plant?"

"They want to cut costs," her father said bitterly.

"You mean the costs of making elevators?"

"Yes. They want to make them with cheaper labor."

"Where do they get cheaper labor?"

"In states where they don't have labor unions."

"So they don't care about people like you who have worked for the company all their lives?

"They don't give a shit about us. All they care about is money."

She refrained from asking the question that was uppermost in her mind.

"The city cleared all that land for them," her father said, "and rearranged the streets for them so they could expand. They got all that money from the government to stay in Yonkers, and now they're leaving to cut costs."

"Don't they have a moral obligation to stay?"

"Of course they do, but the new owners of the company claim they didn't inherit the moral obligation of the previous owners."

"Can't the city do anything about it?"

"All they can do is sue those bastards, which they say they're going to do, but that won't get them anywhere. As usual," he added, "the lawyers will make a lot of money, but the rest of us will be left with nothing."

She finally asked. "So what are you going to do?"

"I'm going to look for another job."

"Are there other jobs like that in Yonkers?"

"Not anymore. The plants have all closed. They've all gone South for cheaper labor."

"Then what kind of job could you get?"

"I'm a good mechanic, so I could get a job repairing things. I'd rather have a job making things, but I'll have to take what I can get."

She felt bad for her father, but she knew he wouldn't appreciate her sympathy, so she didn't offer it. By sitting up straight and holding her head high she let her father know she loved and respected him more than any man in the world.

While her father sat in the living room watching the news on television she went into the kitchen where her mother was preparing dinner. They were having pork chops with applesauce and carrots, which her mother was peeling into the sink. Her mother turned and faced her, and they exchanged a look that conveyed their feelings about what had happened. Then she advanced toward her mother and hugged her.

"Is there anything I can do to help?" she asked her mother.

"You can peel the carrots," her mother said, handing her the peeler.

"I didn't mean that. I meant—"

"I know what you meant. But don't worry. We'll be fine. After what happened to us in the war, this is nothing."

Reassured, she took the peeler, but before starting on the carrots she got a bottle of beer out of the refrigerator, opened it, and took it to her father, which she had done as a little girl every evening after he came home from work. It had been a way of welcoming him, and it had begun with her mother handing her an opened bottle when she was only about five and asking her to take it to her father. Now, receiving the bottle from her, he clasped her hand in appreciation as he had in the past.

While they were eating dinner they didn't talk about Otis Elevator. They talked about her job and her courses, about the new associate pastor at St. Brigid, and about a recent event at the Polish Center. Her parents asked if she had seen Julia, and she admitted that she hadn't. She could tell they weren't happy about Julia's lack of communication, and she resolved to do something about that, though she didn't know what, other than to urge Julia to come with her the next Saturday.

The next day at church she prayed that her father would find a job that gave him satisfaction.

Julia didn't come with her to see their parents until Christmas Eve, when their family had the traditional meatless Wigilia supper. Among other dishes her mother made pickled beets and flounder in a sauce of lemon butter, Ciocia Anna made cheese pierogis and sauerkraut, and Uncle Walter brought herring in wine, cabbage rolls, and poppyseed strudel from a shop on Lockwood Avenue that served the Polish and Ukrainian communities. Again, their uncle and aunt reverted to Polish after they had heard enough about Julia's exploits on Wall Street.

By then her father had a job repairing engines for a bus company. It didn't pay as well as Otis, and it wasn't as challenging, but together with her mother's salary from the phone company it provided enough for them to cover their expenses, so he was happy, and to celebrate he opened a bottle of Wyborowa vodka that he kept in the freezer section of the refrigerator. Uncle Walter had a glass of it, and Marika had a shot of it to share her father's joy, though it was so strong she couldn't finish it.

After dinner they went to midnight Mass at St. Casimir, where Marika enjoyed hearing the Polish Christmas carols sung by the choir. The Mass was as long as usual, and she was exhausted when they got home. That night she had no trouble getting to sleep.

A month later, after coming home from work, Marika got a phone call from her mother informing her that Uncle Walter had died last night from a heart attack. Her mother told her there would be viewings on Thursday at the Polish funeral home on Yonkers Avenue. Her mother, who was going to call Julia, assumed that they would both be there.

Marika didn't have to urge her sister to attend the viewings because Julia had fond memories of Uncle Walter giving her candy when she was a little girl. They met at Grand Central around noon on Thursday and took the train to Yonkers, where their father was waiting for them. While he drove them to the funeral home he answered their questions about Uncle Walter, who had immigrated from Poland in the early 1930s and settled in Yonkers, where like so many other men and women from the Polish community he got his first job at the carpet factory and then embarked on a career with Otis Elevator. Luckily, he had retired with a good pension before the company was acquired by United Technologies.

"What about Ciocia Anna?" Marika asked, concerned that her aunt would now be alone.

"We've asked her to come and live with us."

"Whose room will you give her?" Julia asked.

"We'll give her your room. You hardly ever use it."

"But I have all my stuff in it. I think you should give her Marika's room."

"She can have my room," Marika said, not wanting to have an argument with her sister on the way to the funeral home for the viewing of Uncle Walter.

"Your mother and I will decide which room to give her," their father said as if that was the end of it. And for once Julia didn't argue with him.

They were early for the viewing, which gave Marika an opportunity to kneel at the open casket and pray for the soul of

Uncle Walter. She then went over and comforted her mother, knowing that Uncle Walter had been like a father to her. Though her mother was a strong woman, Marika could tell she was really hurting, so she gave her a long loving hug.

Julia avoided the casket but dutifully got into the receiving line as people began arriving. Most of them were from the Polish community, but there were also colleagues of Uncle Walter from Otis Elevator as well as former colleagues of Ciocia Anna from the railroad, who had various backgrounds. Marika greeted the former in Polish and the latter in English while her sister greeted them all in English.

It was a long day with a viewing from 2:00 to 5:00, an hour break, and then another viewing from 6:00 to 9:00 after which a priest took charge and prayed for the living and the dead in Polish. As they rode home even Julia didn't break the silence.

The funeral Mass was at 10:00 the next morning, celebrated by the same priest, and the burial was at St. Joseph's Cemetery in a plot that Uncle Walter and Ciocia Anna had purchased many years ago. The church was packed, and a lot of people followed the hearse to the cemetery, where the priest said the final prayers. And then at least fifty people went to the Polish Center, where they had a long lunch.

Since the next day was Saturday neither Marika nor Julia had to go to work, so they spent the night at their parents' house, each of them in her own bedroom. There was no further discussion about whose bedroom her parents would give to Ciocia Anna.

They stayed two nights and on Sunday morning they went to Mass with their parents at St. Brigid's and after lunch they went back to the city.

On the way, sitting in an almost empty car of the train, Julia said: "You know, I was thinking. Uncle Walter and Ciocia Anna lived in a community, and our parents live in a community, but I don't think I'll ever live in a community."

"You never know," Marika said. "When they came here from Poland they didn't have a community."

"But they found a community."

"So maybe you'll find a community."

"Yeah, maybe I will. But right now I can't imagine one."

"It's different for us," Marika said, "but we have a lot of advantages that they didn't have. So we should be thankful."

"I know we should," Julia said, bleakly staring out the window of the train. "But you have more to be thankful for than I do."

"I do? Why?"

"You're pretty, and everyone likes you."

"I'm not that pretty, and not everyone likes me."

"Mommy and Daddy like you better than they like me."

"Oh, that's not true," Marika said. "Our parents love us both equally."

"They love you more. And you know why? Because you're what they wanted, and I'm not at all what they wanted."

"Where did you get that idea?"

"I got it from them, from the way they treat us differently."

"They treat us differently because we're different. But they love us equally."

"Well, I don't feel they do."

"But that's your feeling, not theirs, and you're projecting it onto them."

"I'm not projecting it onto them. I know how they feel."

"You can't know how they feel," Marika said. "You can only imagine how they feel."

"Since when are you an expert on other people's feelings?"

"I'm not an expert. I just pay attention to other people, and I imagine how they feel. But I can still be wrong about them."

"When were you ever wrong about anyone?"

"I was wrong about a guy I thought about marrying."

"What guy?" Julia said as if she didn't believe there ever was such a guy.

"A guy I dated for more than a year."

"Why haven't I heard of him?"

"You were still living at home, and I was living in the city. So we didn't see each other much. In any case, I was wrong about him."

Julia was silent for a while, and then she said: "I still feel that Mommy and Daddy love you more than they love me."

"As I said, that's your feeling, not theirs."

When her sister didn't argue further Marika inferred that at least Julia might consider the possibility that she was projecting her feeling onto their parents.

A few weeks later she found a packet of fliers in the vestibule of her apartment building. She took one and read it while waiting for the elevator. It was promoting an exercise class that was being offered only a few blocks away. She had thought about doing something to stay in shape, and since her evenings during the week were free except on Tuesdays and Thursdays, when she had classes at Hunter, she decided to look into the exercise class, so after Evelyn came home from work she showed her the flier.

"I've heard about this class," Evelyn said. "A girl at work has been taking it for years, and she swears by it."

"Do you want to try it?" Marika asked, preferring to go to the class with someone.

"Yeah, why not. I need to get into better shape. The girl at work says the classes take about an hour, and she goes twice a week."

According to the flier there were classes at 5:00, 6:15, and 7:30 on weekdays, and at 10:00 and 11:15 on Saturdays, so they agreed to go to the 6:15 class on Wednesday.

Wearing sweatpants and sweatshirts under winter coats they walked to the address given by the flier. It was a four-story building in the middle of the block off Second Avenue, across from a school. After being admitted to the building by a buzzer they went through an open door and were met by a red-haired girl at a reception desk, who explained that a trial class was free, and if they liked it they could sign up for ten or twenty classes. The girl told them mats were provided, and she advised them to wear lighter clothes like yoga pants and tee shirts in the future. She added that there were changing rooms upstairs so they didn't have to come to class in their exercise clothes.

Since they were early for the class they could choose their spots on the floor of a room that must have been the living and dining area of a duplex apartment. A tall lean woman with dark hair fastened back with a clip was standing at the front of the room, and after introducing herself as their instructor she suggested that they set down their mats in the front and center, so they could get the attention they needed as new students.

The instructor, whose name was Kelsi, explained that the exercises were developed by the physical trainer of dancers in the Joffrey Ballet, so they were rigorous, and they emphasized strengthening the core, limbering the back, and stretching the hip and leg muscles. As other students came into the room bringing their mats they were welcomed by Kelsi, who knew not only their names but also things about them so that she could make references to their jobs or their relationships.

Gently but firmly, with a clear voice, Kelsi warmed them up and guided them through the exercises, which were indeed rigorous. They demanded a lot of stretching, and Kelsi reminded the students to go beyond what was comfortable but not to go until they felt pain. She gave special attention to Marika and Evelyn, adjusting their positions and making sure that they breathed correctly, inhaling when they relaxed muscles and exhaling when they tensed them. At one point Kelsi laid her hands gently on Marika's shoulders, feeling the muscles and saying: "You're very tense. It feels like you're bracing yourself for disaster. So try to relax."

Knowing that Kelsi was right about her tension, Marika did try to relax, and eventually she got into the rhythm of breathing: when she breathed out she expelled anxieties, and when she breathed in she inhaled peace. About halfway through the class she finally relaxed and began to enjoy the exercises, letting her body do the work and letting her mind take a welcome break.

When the class was over Kelsi praised them for doing so well their first time, and she told them she hoped they would continue taking classes. They both agreed that they had liked the class, and they both signed up for ten classes. And on the way home they resisted the temptation to stop at a bar for a glass or two of wine, not wanting to replenish the calories that they had worked so hard to burn off.

All through that spring they dutifully went to exercise classes two evenings a week and to classes at Hunter two evenings a week, which still left them plenty of time for doing assignments in their courses. By the middle of May they completed the last required courses for the master's program, leaving only the thesis to do, and they celebrated by going to a bar that served margaritas in enormous balloon glasses.

On a Monday toward the end of May, when she and Evelyn walked into the exercise class they noticed a new, unusual student lying on a mat in the front and center. What made this student unusual was that he was a guy, and until now there hadn't been any guys in the classes. Marika's first reaction was that having a guy in the class would spoil things, though she couldn't explain exactly how. It was just that with girls, only girls, she felt at ease in yoga pants and a tee shirt doing stretches and leg lifts and rollups and splits, whereas she would feel self-conscious doing such things with her body in the presence of a guy. But there was nothing she could do about it, so she and Evelyn set their mats down in a row behind the unwelcome guy.

As soon as they were in the starting position where you sat up straight with your legs stretched out in front of you, she noticed that the guy had perfect posture, and from then on she couldn't help glancing at him from time to time to see how he was doing the exercises. She had to admit he was doing them well, so well that she wondered if he was a dancer or an instructor from another studio who had come to see how Kelsi was conducting her class. On the last exercise, where you stood tall with your palms pressed together, raising your head until your feet almost left the floor, she noticed how impressively tall the guy stood.

When he turned around at the end of the class she saw his face for the first time, and she liked everything about it. She especially liked the kind eyes, the generous mouth, and the strong chin. He was a good-looking guy, with a good body, but most important he looked like a good person.

"Hey, are you coming?" Evelyn said.

"Oh, yeah," she said in a daze. She bent over and picked up her mat and followed Evelyn out of the room, not looking back.

They stopped at the desk and turned in their mats, and then they headed out of the building. They were on the sidewalk, walking toward Second Avenue, when Evelyn asked: "Did you like having a guy in the class?"

"At first I didn't like it," she said. "But I got used to it. And he did the exercises so well that I wondered if he was a dancer."

"He could be. He has a good body."

"But I don't think he looks like a dancer." By now they had learned that the instructors were typically dancers.

"You mean he doesn't look gay?"

"No, I don't think he does."

"So maybe he just came to the class to meet a girl."

"Oh, I don't think so," Marika said. "A guy like that wouldn't have to come to an exercise class to meet a girl."

"A guy like what?" Evelyn asked her playfully.

"A good-looking guy with a good body."

"Mm. Then why did that guy come to our class?"

"Maybe for the same reason that we do—to keep in shape."

"Yeah, maybe." Evelyn paused. "Do you like him?"

"What? How could I like him? I don't even know him."

"Well, you couldn't take your eyes off him."

"I was curious" Marika said. "He's the first guy we've had in the class. And I wasn't the only one who was curious."

"No, you weren't," Evelyn agreed. "He got a lot of attention from the ladies."

That night, lying awake in bed, Marika tried not to think about the guy, but his face kept coming back into her mind. And she wondered if she would see him again. If he was a dancer he had other ways of keeping in shape. Or if he was an instructor he might have been there only one time to see how Kelsi conducted the class. Or if was doing a trial class he might decide it wasn't challenging enough for him and not come back. As usual, she lowered her expectations so she wouldn't be disappointed if he didn't come back.

When they went to class on Wednesday he was already there lying on a mat in the same location. Marika moved to the far left side of the second row so she wouldn't be distracted by him, and she concentrated on doing the exercises as if he wasn't there.

As she and Evelyn were leaving the building after class she had a sense that they were being followed, so she turned around, and it was the guy.

"Yeah, I was following you," he said with a smile. "When I talked with Kelsi about signing up for more classes, I told her I wanted to get opinions from students who'd taken classes for a while, and she referred me to you."

"She did?" Evelyn said doubtfully.

"So how long have you been taking classes?"

"Oh, I don't know. Four or five months."

"Does it help you stay in shape?"

"Yeah. I think it does."

He looked at Marika, who hadn't said a word. "Do you plan to keep taking them?"

"Yeah," she said. "I think it's worth the time and money."

Evelyn moved to resume walking.

"Would you like to have a drink?" he asked them.

"I'd love to," Evelyn said, "but I have a date for dinner, so maybe next time. I mean if you keep taking classes."

"What about you?" he asked Marika.

"Well—" she hesitated. She wanted to have a drink with him, but she was still wary after her experience with Thayer.

"Go ahead," Evelyn urged her.

The guy gazed at her with hope in his eyes.

"Okay," she finally said. "But I can't stay long."

The three of them walked together up Second Avenue until they came to a bar where she and Evelyn often hung out, and Marika stopped there, wanting to have a drink in a place that was familiar.

"Is this a good place?" the guy asked.

"Yeah," she said.

"I'll see you later," Evelyn said, leaving them.

The guy held the door for her, and she went in and headed to the end of the bar where she and Evelyn usually sat. The bartender greeted her, and he took their orders: a white wine for her and a red wine for him.

"Is this where you guys hang out?"

"Yeah. We like it here."

He paused for a moment. "What's your name?"

"Marika," she said.

"Marika," he said as if he liked the name.

"It's a Polish name."

"Well, my name is Frank, and it could be any kind of name, but in my case it's Italian. My real name is Franco."

"Like Franco Zeffirelli?"

"Yeah, though I'm not so famous."

"I'm not so famous either."

He paused for a moment again. "Where do you work?"

"I work at a small publishing company."

"What do you do there?"

"I edit books."

"What kind of books?"

"Mostly trade books." Since he looked as if he didn't know what she meant she explained: "Not textbooks, but books that people read for pleasure."

"You didn't read your textbooks for pleasure?"

She smiled. "No. But I didn't mind reading them because I had a purpose."

"What was your purpose?"

"To get a degree."

At that point the bartender set their glasses of wine on the bar in front of them and then returned to the girl he had been talking with when they came in.

After a long sip of wine Frank resumed their conversation, asking: "Where did you go to college?"

"Fordham. Where did you go?"

"I went to Manhattan."

"So you're an engineer?"

"Yeah, I'm a civil engineer."

"Where do you work?"

"I work at a large company that provides services for real estate projects."

"You mean like office buildings and housing projects?"

"Yeah. I work on environmental impact statements. So what was your major at Fordham?" he asked, changing the subject back to her.

"English. And I'm about to complete a master's in English at Hunter College."

"Really? I'll bet your parents are proud of you."

"They are. I'm the first person in my family to go to college."

"I was the first in my family."

"Where are you from?"

"Yonkers," he said.

"You're kidding," she said. "I'm from Yonkers too."

"What part of Yonkers?"

"I grew up on Nodine Hill, but then my parents moved to northwest Yonkers, off North Broadway. What part of Yonkers are you from?"

"Southeast Yonkers, off Kimball Avenue."

"So we're from opposite sides of the compass."

He smiled. "Yeah. Is that a problem?"

"I don't know. At least we're both from Yonkers, so we have that in common."

"I think we have more than that in common," he said, gazing at her with admiration.

A little flustered, she took a sip of wine, reminding herself to go slow. She liked this guy, she liked him a lot but she didn't want to get hurt again.

They stayed for another round of wine, and from talking with him she learned that his father did renovations of houses, that after high school he had enlisted in the marines, and that he had served for five years, including a tour of duty in Vietnam. He had gone to Manhattan College on the GI Bill, and one of his professors had recommended him to the company where he worked now. He had moved to Manhattan three years ago, and he lived in an old tenement building on East 82nd Street between York and East End. When she revealed that she lived on East 80th Street between Second and First Avenues, he wondered aloud why they hadn't met before. He was sure they hadn't passed each other on the street because he would have noticed her. She didn't say it, but she was also sure she would have noticed him.

They ended up having dinner together. He suggested moving to a booth, but she said she was fine sitting at the bar. They had hamburgers, which she had recommended, and they hung out there until almost ten. He walked her home, and stopping at the entrance of her building she was afraid that he would try to kiss her, but he didn't, so she was both relieved and disappointed. Before they parted they exchanged business cards, and he said he would call her.

When she entered her apartment Evelyn was still up, sitting on the sofa and cutting her toenails. With a meaningful look Evelyn said: "So he's not gay?"

She laughed. "No. He's a former marine."

"I should have guessed. He looks like a marine."

She understood that Evelyn meant this as a compliment. "He didn't come to our exercise class to meet a girl. He came to keep in shape."

"Well, he did meet a girl."

"Yeah, he did." She opened her pocketbook and took out his business card and perused it, saying: "And I met a guy."

"What's his name?"

"Franco Bonetti."

"That sounds like a guy who played for the Rangers."

She wasn't a hockey fan, so she didn't know. All she knew was that she liked him and she hoped he would call her.

SIX

THE DOCTOR FOUND them in the waiting area and gave them an update on Jessica. She was still in a coma, but her signs were good and the prognosis was good. They asked him some questions, which he did his best to answer, but they were left wondering how long it would take for Jessica to come out of the coma. They went into her room, and they stayed there as long as the nurse allowed. Before they left she kissed Jessica on the forehead, saying "I love you" and hoping she heard it.

After two visits to the hospital that day they were too exhausted to cook dinner, so they ordered a pizza to be delivered, and they ate it at the kitchen table. They had held off calling Nina and letting her know about Jessica because they didn't have anything positive to tell her, but they agreed it was time to call Nina and tell her what they did know.

Nina answered after the first ring.

"Hi, it's Mom," Marika said. "I hope you're not eating now."

"No, I'm about to start cooking dinner," Nina said. "What's happening?"

"Well, we didn't want to worry you, but yesterday Jessica was taken to the emergency room at St. John's Hospital. She had an overdose of a drug, and it put her into a coma, but the doctor said the prognosis is good. She's in the ICU now."

"Oh, my God. What kind of drug?"

"The doctor said it was fentanyl."

"Shit. How did she get it?"

"We don't know. It was probably from someone she met on the internet. And I don't think she knew she was taking it."

"I don't think so either," Nina said. "So when can I see her?"

"We're hoping she'll come out of the coma soon, so you can see her then."

"Okay. Just let me know, and I can come there after work." There was a pause, and then Nina said softly: "Poor Jess. I'll pray for her."

"Thanks. I love you."

"I love you too."

After the phone call she was even more exhausted than before, so she went up to bed, leaving Frank in the living room, where he was watching the news on television.

She hoped she would drop off to sleep right away, but she lay awake, worrying about Jessica and remembering events that had led to this situation. But it wasn't long before her mind wandered back to the time when she and Frank were dating.

Frank called her at work the day after they had met, and he invited her for dinner that night. He took her to a restaurant on Second Avenue where he introduced her to Italian food. After asking if there was anything she didn't like or couldn't eat he ordered a three-course meal for them: melon with prosciutto, linguine with artichoke hearts, and veal scallopine with wild mushrooms, accompanied by a bottle of white wine. Since pizza and spaghetti with meatballs were the only Italian foods she had known, the meal opened up a whole new cuisine for her. Of course it wasn't only the food, it was also the company that she enjoyed, and they lingered at the table after a desert of tiramisu, sipping sambuca.

They didn't stop talking the whole time. They talked about food, about their families, about their jobs, about whatever came to mind, moving from one topic to another with pauses to eat or sip wine, and by the time they left the restaurant Marika felt as if she had known Frank all her life. He walked her home, and at the entrance of her building he leaned toward her and kissed her gently, not provocatively, as if he somehow understood her need to go slow.

For the next few weeks they had drinks on Wednesday after exercise class and dinner on Friday, usually at an Italian restaurant but once at a Czech restaurant where she introduced him to Eastern European cuisine (there wasn't a Polish restaurant in the neighborhood). He always walked her home, and at the entrance of her building he always kissed her goodnight without any hint of going further, which she appreciated, believing that they would both know the right time for them to make love.

A month later Marika completed her thesis for the master's program. The subject was Joseph Conrad, and she focused on how his Polish background had influenced his short stories. Her mentor praised it and gave her an A, and a few weeks later she received her degree. At this point she didn't have any clear idea of what she would do with this degree, but at least it got her a small salary increase from the publishing company.

In the meantime Evelyn's boyfriend, now her fiancé, had begun working for PepsiCo at its head office in Westchester, so he no longer worked on Saturdays, and she had begun spending the weekend at his apartment. They were planning to get married in October. The wedding was going to be in Rochester, where Evelyn was from, and she wanted Marika to be her maid of honor. Not having a driver's license Marika couldn't rent a car and drive to Rochester, but the problem of how to get to the wedding was solved by a colleague of Evelyn who was going to be a bridesmaid and planned to drive to Rochester. Since the colleague lived in Tarrytown with her parents, Marika would only have to take the train and meet her at the Tarrytown station, so she agreed to be the maid of honor at Evelyn's wedding.

Her other, more important problem was finding a roommate to replace Evelyn. She had heard horror stories about girls who put ads in the paper to find a roommate, so she didn't want to do that, which left her relying on word of mouth. The colleague of Evelyn who was going to drive her to Rochester might have been a good candidate, but it turned out that she had already lined up another situation. Marika finally decided it would be safe to post an ad on the bulletin board at her office, where there were ads for summer rentals in the Hamptons and on the Jersey Shore, and that generated a few responses, including one from a girl who worked for the same acquiring editor. She didn't know the girl very well, but from meetings in the office and conversations in the women's room, she knew her well enough to consider her as a roommate, so they had lunch at a nearby coffee shop to talk about the possibility.

The girl's name was Tina, short for Valentina, and she was Puerto Rican. She had a bachelor's degree in English from City College, and she had started working for the company a year after Marika. She lived with her parents in the Barrio around 116th Street, where she had grown up, and she would have continued living with them if they hadn't decided to move to Florida. She had visited Florida with them, and she didn't like it. She wanted to stay in New York, but on her salary she couldn't afford the rent on any of the apartments she had looked at, so it was a major attraction that Marika's apartment was under rent control. It didn't take Marika long to decide that Tina would be a good roommate. She liked her, and she could tell she was responsible. The only hitch was that her parents wanted her to move to Florida with them, and if she was going to stay in New York she would have to get their approval of the apartment and the roommate. So the next Saturday afternoon her parents came to inspect the apartment and interview the roommate.

Her parents spoke to Marika in formal, accented English, and she could tell they were very conservative. She hoped they could tell she was well raised, and she thought it helped when they saw a picture of the Blessed Mother that her mother had cut from a calendar and framed for her to hang on the wall of her bedroom. Before making any decision Tina's parents went out into the hall, where Marika could hear them having a serious discussion in Spanish, but when they came back they were smiling and they gave their approval to Tina, who later told her that the picture in her bedroom had helped.

Since Evelyn wouldn't be moving out until October and was only gone for weekends with her fiancé, Marika continued her life as usual, going to exercise class twice a week, having drinks with Frank after exercise class on Wednesday, and having dinner with him on Friday. She was still going to Yonkers on Saturday and spending the night with her parents, and Frank didn't object to that because he spent Saturday night with his parents. They both went by subway, and it wasn't long before they synchronized their schedules and took the subway together. That was how they met each other's father, and how their fathers also met, picking them up at the Woodlawn station.

One Friday, after they had gone to the Czech restaurant, he walked her home and kissed her goodnight as usual. By then she was ready, so she kissed him back in a way that let him know she was ready, and he responded in a way that let her know he had gotten the message. Trusting him, she said: "Would you like to come in for a drink?"

"Yeah, but what about your roommate?"

"She's spending the night with her fiancé."

"Well, then okay."

She unlocked the outer door and led him into the building.

In the elevator, riding up to the third floor, they resumed kissing, and by the time they entered her apartment she no longer thought about having a drink. She headed directly for her bedroom, and he followed her.

Afterward she fell asleep with her face against the back of his neck and an arm draped over his waist, and she didn't wake up until the morning.

From then on the major change in their routine was that after dinner on Friday they spent the night in her apartment. They had breakfast together, and then he went home to do laundry and other chores. Later that morning they met at the subway entrance on 86th Street for the trip to Woodlawn. Of course her mother, having learned about Frank from her father, wanted to meet him, so they finally arranged to have dinner with both sets of parents at an Italian restaurant on Bronx River Road.

The restaurant was in a strip mall, and from the outside it didn't look like much, but inside it was packed and buzzing. Frank's parents were already seated at a table that his father had reserved for them, and while they introduced themselves Marika could tell that their parents were going to hit it off. Their fathers both worked with their hands, her father with machines and his father with building materials, and their mothers both worked for large companies, her mother with the phone company and his mother with the electric company. Both families had two children, her family two girls and his family two boys. And both families were practicing Catholics, her family going to St. Brigid and his family going to St. Frances. So they had a lot in common, and they had a lot to talk about.

Frank's father, who knew the owner of the restaurant, ordered a bottle of white wine for the women and a bottle of red wine for the men. He recommended everything, but in particular the steak, the fish, and the zuppa di pesce. Marika had sole livornese, and Frank had zuppa di pesce, which somehow he finished. They were having dessert when the lights dimmed and a scratched record started playing "Happy Birthday." The waiters, singing in a group, headed for a random table with one of them carrying a cake but at the last minute they swerved and went to the table where the person having the birthday was seated. Everyone applauded, with a few whistles, and the birthday woman, who looked like a grandmother, blew out the candles.

The owner brought a bottle of sambuca, which they passed around the table and poured into brandy glasses. Raising his glass, Frank's father said: "*Alla salute!*"

"*Alla salute!*" they all said.

"How do you say that in Polish?" Frank's mother asked.

"*Na zdrowie!*" Marika's father said.

"Nasdrovia!" they repeated.

On the way out of the restaurant Marika heard her mother say to Frank's mother: "We really enjoyed the evening."

"We did too," his mother said. "We have to get together again."

Their exchange made Marika feel that she and Frank already had their parents' blessing.

In the car on their way home her father said: "I like that young man. I understand that he was a marine."

"Yeah, he served for five years."

"Good for him. We need more young men like him."

And that made Marika glow.

As the weeks passed her relationship with Frank deepened, and she was already thinking of marrying him by the time she went to Evelyn's wedding in October. It was a long trip to Rochester, but she and Evelyn's colleague didn't run out of things to talk about. The colleague was in a serious relationship with a guy, whom she was thinking of marrying, so mostly they talked about their boyfriends. The dinner the night before the wedding, the wedding, and the reception were happy experiences that advanced their thoughts of getting married, as they agreed in their conversation on the way home.

Back in the city she helped Tina move into the apartment, and though she should have been tired from the trip she stayed up late, hanging out with her new roommate.

In the morning she woke up smelling coffee, and she found Tina in the kitchenette preparing breakfast. It was Monday, so they both had to go to work, but they had time to eat the sweet bread and drink the strong coffee that Tina provided.

"The bread is called pan de Mallorca," Tina explained. "It's Puerto Rican."

"I love it. Did you make it?"

"No. I bought it at a bakery in the Barrio."

"What about the coffee?"

"It's Puerto Rican coffee," Tina said. "Do you like it?"

"Yeah. It's stronger than American coffee, but it's really good on a Monday morning."

Together, they walked to the subway station on 77th Street, and they talked about their boss, a woman in her early forties who had a master's degree from Columbia. They both respected her, and they had both learned a lot from her, but Tina wished she would loosen up.

They went home together on the subway, and since she was going to exercise class Tina offered to make dinner for them. She wasn't going to do anything with Frank after class, so she accepted the offer. And when she returned to the apartment after class she was greeted by the smell of roast chicken, which Tina served with rice and beans.

While they were eating they agreed to share the tasks of food shopping and preparing meals. Except for Wednesday and Friday when she had dinner with Frank, and Saturday when she had dinner with her parents, she was home for dinner. And since Tina didn't have a current boyfriend she was home most nights, though she had a sister in Queens and friends in Manhattan whom she saw now and then.

Before they were done eating dinner Marika invited Tina to join her in the exercise class on Wednesday so she could try it, and Tina accepted the invitation. Tina did like it, and she signed up for ten classes. As they left the studio Marika knew that Frank wouldn't mind if she invited Tina to join them for a drink, and they sat in a booth, where they had drinks and eventually hamburgers. Frank was nice to Tina, and he was impressed when he learned that her father had served in the marines, with active duty in Korea.

Now that she had a roommate who was at the apartment on Friday, she couldn't have Frank come home with her after dinner, so they started going to his apartment. As he had warned her, it was a five-floor walkup but if you went up the stairs slowly it wasn't too bad, and when you arrived you were in an apartment with five large rooms, all in a row, which is why it was called a railroad flat. There was space in the kitchen for a refrigerator, a stove, an immense sink, and a table that would seat eight people, plus a sitting area that looked out into a green area between the buildings. The bathroom, which was off the kitchen, had an ancient tub with a shower rigged above it and a toilet on a raised platform with a pull chain. The next room off the kitchen was a bedroom with a queen size bed, the next room a walk-through closet, the next room a study with a drafting table, and the last room a living room with a sofa, two chairs, and a sideboard. On her tour through the apartment Marika paused at the drafting table where she saw a pen-and-ink drawing of a city street scene.

"Did you do that?" she asked Frank.

"Yeah, that's what I do in my spare time."

"It's very good. Did you take classes in drawing?"

"No, but I took classes in drafting. To be an engineer you have to be able to draft."

"Well, I really like it. I wish I had a talent for art or music."

"You have a talent for life," he told her. "That's the most important thing."

Since Tina's parents had moved to Florida and her only remaining family in New York was her sister, who was married and lived in Queens, Marika thought of inviting her to Yonkers on a Saturday, which she did after making sure that Julia wouldn't be there. So on that Saturday she and Tina took the subway together (Frank was doing something else that night), and her father met them at the Woodlawn station.

Her father, who liked women, liked Tina immediately, and after listening to them talk with each other Marika had the feeling that her father would have liked to have a daughter more like Tina. They stopped at the house, and then with her mother and Ciocia Anna they went to the Chart House in Dobbs Ferry and sat at a table with a view of the river, though it was dark and what you could see were mainly lights reflecting off the still water.

Julia's bedroom was occupied now by Ciocia Anna, so that night Marika shared her bedroom with Tina. They talked for a while lying in the dark, and before going to sleep Marika wished her sister was more like Tina.

She invited Tina to have Thanksgiving dinner with her family, but Tina was going to her sister's house in Queens to celebrate what they called Día de Acción de Gracias.

Over the next few weeks she and Tina went Christmas shopping together. She had to buy presents for her mother, her father, her sister, and her aunt, and since she had ideas about what they needed it wasn't a challenge to find things for them. But it was a challenge to find something for Frank, and she considered several possibilities before deciding to buy him a special pen for drawing, which she found in a shop for art supplies.

On Christmas Eve she and Frank took the subway together to Woodlawn, and on the way they exchanged presents, which they agreed not to open until the next morning. His present to her was professionally wrapped and came in a bag from Bloomingdale's, so she guessed that it was something to wear, and she wondered what it was.

Before sitting down at the dining room table her family followed the tradition of breaking opłatek, a wafer similar to a communion host. Marika's father began the ceremony, breaking off a piece of the wafer and giving it to her mother with a prayer. Her mother then broke off a piece and gave it to Ciocia Anna with a prayer. The opłatek went around the table, with each of them breaking off a piece and saying a prayer. When it came around to Marika she broke off a piece and gave it to Julia with a prayer of thanks for her family and a blessing for her sister.

The Wigilia supper was actually supposed to have twelve courses, which represented the Twelve Apostles, but as far back as Marika could remember they had never made an exact count of the courses. That year the first courses were pickled beets and herring in wine, which her father being from the Baltic especially liked. They were followed by a hearty soup made with wild and domestic mushrooms, which everyone liked. Then came a platter of sauteed flounder with a sauce of butter, lemon juice, fresh dill, and chopped hard-boiled eggs, accompanied by cheese pierogi, braised sauerkraut, cabbage rolls stuffed with rice in tomato sauce, and warm potato salad. The meal ended with Christmas bread and poppyseed strudel. While they were eating the bread and the strudel her father passed around a pitcher of honey-spiced vodka. Marika poured a little vodka, which she sipped, while Julia poured a lot, which she chugged.

Later they went to midnight Mass at St. Casimir, which as usual could have been warmer but knowing what to expect they were dressed for it. As she looked around the church, which was filled, Marika recognized people from their old neighborhood who were mostly around her parents' age, but there were also young people who could have been recent immigrants, wearing leather jackets and scarves. As usual the Mass was in Polish, and the choir up in the mezzanine above the entrance sang the Kolędy that she remembered, including *"Dzisiaj w Betlejem,"* *"Wśród Nocnej Ciszy,"* and *"Lulajże Jezuniu,"* which they sang twice. It was her favorite carol, and in a soft voice she sang along with the choir. When the Mass was ended she joined in the recessional hymn and left the church with a feeling of peace.

She shared her bedroom with Julia, who was less talkative than usual, so Marika wasn't kept awake listening to her sister. She slept well, and in the morning she couldn't wait to open the present from Frank. It was a gray cashmere sweater that she had admired weeks ago while passing through Bloomingdale's with him. What really touched her was his noticing that she liked the sweater and going back to buy it for her. And since she loved sweaters it was the best present he could have gotten for her.

When she returned to her apartment that evening Tina, who had spent Christmas with her sister, told her there was a message from Frank. She called him right away and thanked him for the sweater, and he thanked her for the pen. As they talked on the phone she envisioned the possibility of being married to him by next Christmas.

Her company gave Marika two weeks of vacation per year which she had never used for travel, mainly because she couldn't afford it on her salary. Before moving to the city she had spent her vacations with her family, helping her mother around the house, and during her years of living in the city she had spent her vacations sleeping late, trying new recipes, reading novels, and doing things to improve the apartment. But this year she thought about going on a trip, and when she suggested it to Frank he liked the idea and asked where she would like to go. She had never been out of the country, and since it was the middle of a cold winter she told him she would like to go somewhere warm, but not Florida. And he told her he would find a place.

It didn't take him long to find Tortola, which he learned about from an agent near his office. Tortola was in the British Virgin Islands, and it was known for boating and unspoiled beaches. You got there by flying to Puerto Rico on a commercial jet and then taking a small plane to Tortola. The agent recommended a resort on Long Bay that had twenty rooms and five-star food, so after seeing a photo showing its view of a white sandy beach and a turquoise bay, and hearing its price for a whole week, which included food and lodging, she asked Frank to go ahead and make reservations. Her only question had been about the plane from Puerto Rico to Tortola, and Frank had assured her that it would be a DC3, a reliable plane that had been in service for more than forty years.

Since she had never been on a plane before, the trip to San Juan was a whole new experience, and she was anxious as they waited on the runway of JFK in a line of planes that were going to take off. She blessed herself and held Frank's hand while the plane raced down the runway, and she gave thanks when they were finally lifted off the ground.

When they landed almost three hours later she was relieved to get out of the plane and out of the terminal into the warm tropical air, which smelled of flowers and ripening fruit. They got a taxi, which took them to a hotel that overlooked the ocean. After checking in, she grabbed her suitcase with the intention of carrying it to their room, but a bellhop told her to leave it, he would take care of it. Not trusting him, she reluctantly left her suitcase with him and walked to the elevator with Frank. The number of their room indicated that they were on the fourth floor, so they went there but couldn't find the room, so they went back down and eventually found their room two floors below the lobby. It was a nice room, with a balcony and a view of the ocean, but she couldn't relax until the bellhop brought their luggage.

Frank gently kidded her about not trusting the bellhop, and she explained that it was in her culture not to trust people because over the centuries Poland had been repeatedly invaded by barbarian hordes who raped the women and killed the men and devastated the countryside. The most recent barbarians were the Germans and the Russians, whom her parents had escaped from. And the Russians were still occupying Poland as a colony.

Frank understood, and he gave her a reassuring hug before

suggesting that they go to the patio and have a drink. It was on the patio, smelling the ocean and hearing the regular sound of the surf, where she saw her first lizard and had her first piña colada. With the help of the rum she finally relaxed.

They had dinner in the hotel restaurant and afterward they went to the lounge where a live band was playing Latin music. For a while they sat at a table and watched other people dancing, and then Frank suggested that they try dancing even though they didn't know how to do the salsa or whatever it was. So they got up and tried to imitate what the other people were doing, and they had a good time. When the band played a slow song they held each other tight and swayed with the music, sliding their feet.

The next morning they went to the airport for their flight to Tortola. They were at the gate when Marika noticed a tiny plane in front of them.

"Is that a DC3?" she asked.

"No, it's a small plane," Frank told her. "Don't worry. It's not our plane."

But it *was* their plane, the airline having cancelled the larger plane for a lack of passengers. Marika held Frank's hand as he led her across the tarmac and up the stairs into a plane that only had seats for four passengers plus the pilot. An older couple boarded ahead of them, so she and Frank had to sit directly behind the pilot, a stolid man with a brushy mustache.

Marika found the seat belt and buckled it for dear life. She prayed continuously as the pilot taxied down the runway, turned around, and then revved the engine. She closed her eyes and squeezed Frank's hand and fervently prayed: *"Drogi Boże, daj nam bezpiecznie dotrzeć."*

After going almost to the end of the runway the plane finally took off, and Marika said a prayer of thanks. She didn't relax, but she did find the courage to look down at the ocean, which wasn't far below them. In fact, they were so close to the water that she could distinguish two men on a fishing boat who could have been father and son.

The pilot had to suspend his first attempt to land because there was a herd of goats on the runway, and when they finally did land Marika felt like kneeling on the ground and giving thanks. She couldn't help blaming Frank for putting her through this ordeal, but she knew it wasn't his fault that the airline had switched planes, so by the time they left the rustic terminal and spotted a taxi she had forgiven him.

Their room at the resort had everything she could have wanted: a queen size bed, a clean bathroom, a chest of drawers, and an ample closet with plastic hangers. She needed time to unpack and get settled, but she was ready to go and have a drink when Frank, after patiently waiting for her, suggested it.

There was a bar on a patio that overlooked the beach, which looked as good as it had in the pictures. They gazed at it for a while, and then they sat down at a white metal table. She ordered a piña colada, and the server brought a whole pineapple with its top cut off. With a knife he cut around inside it and then poured rum and finally coconut milk into the pineapple, mixed it with the knife, and said: "This is a natural piña colada. I hope you like it."

She did like it, and it wasn't long before she was joking with Frank about the plane that had looked like a mosquito. And he admitted that he had been nervous until he saw the pilot with his brushy mustache, probably a veteran of the Royal Air Force.

The dining room wasn't large enough to accommodate all the guests, so there were two seatings. Most people evidently preferred the second seating because all the tables were booked for it, but since she was feeling a little drained by their trip Marika was happy to have dinner at the first seating, at six o'clock. The food was delicious: for the main course they gave you a choice of fish or meat, and she had the fish, a grouper in coconut cream sauce. They had plenty of time to eat a three-course dinner leisurely and vacate their table for the second seating. At that point they headed for the lounge, where they sat at a table and ordered sambucas.

At the table next to them was a couple in their mid-thirties. The woman started a conversation by saying: "You guys look familiar. Have I seen you in movies?"

"Movies? Us?" Marika laughed. "No, we're just ordinary people."

"Oh, come on. You must be somebody."

"Well, I'm Marika. I'm a Polish girl from Yonkers."

"I'm Frank. I'm an Italian guy from Yonkers."

"Yonkers?" the man said as if he had heard of it. "That's near New York City, isn't it?"

"Yeah, it is," Marika said. "It's just north of New York City. Where are you guys from?"

"We're from Toronto," the woman said. "I'm Shirley."

"And I'm Ben," the man said.

They talked for quite a while exchanging information, and then the woman said: "We're leaving tomorrow, so we can share our secret with you."

"Secret?" Marika said, interested.

"If you walk down the beach until after the bend, you have complete privacy. In fact, if you want you can skinny dip."

"You mean at night?"

"No, during the day. There's no one around to see you."

"It's a lot of fun," the man said.

"If we weren't leaving," the woman said, "we wouldn't tell you because we'd want to keep that part of the beach all to ourselves. But we're leaving tomorrow, so you can have it."

"Well, thank you," Marika said, uncertain about the value of this legacy because she couldn't imagine herself skinny dipping on a beach. She was even too reserved to wear a two-piece swimsuit. But the couple didn't seem wild and crazy, they seemed like normal people, and they were nice to share their secret.

After a good night's sleep Marika got up and took a shower. She was using the hair drier provided by the resort when Frank returned after going to find out where breakfast was served. When she was ready they went to the patio where they had drinks yesterday, and they had an English breakfast, which included kippers, sausages, and baked tomatoes. They spent a few hours sitting by the pool, where an athletic guy was doing laps, and then they decided to change into their swimsuits and go to the beach.

The beach was on a long bay that extended from a mile or so before the resort to several miles after it to a distant point of land on which you could see what looked like another resort. Between the two resorts there was nothing, there were no houses, no hotels, no buildings of any kind. Around the bend you couldn't see either resort. This section of the beach was out of sight except by someone who might happen to be walking by there, and the Canadians had assured them that in their experience of frequent skinny dipping no one ever walked by there.

Marika of course would never think of skinny dipping, but she did want to go into the water, so she put her towel down on the beach and walked to the edge. The waves were mild because as Frank had learned from the agent the bay was sheltered by a reef, which made it safe to swim. And Marika felt safe as she waded into the placid water, which was warm enough to be comfortable and cool enough to be refreshing.

Frank joined her, and they waded out until the water was up to their waists. She had learned to swim at Orchard Beach in the Bronx, where her family had gone several times every summer when she was growing up, but she only knew how to stay afloat and how to do the sidestroke, which as soon as it was deep enough she started doing, heading out a little further. Frank was swimming on his back, which he said was good for long distances if you were ever lost at sea. She assumed that this was something he had learned in the marines.

They swam for a while, and then they headed in. As they were standing at the edge of the beach Frank looked around and then he said: "You want to try it?"

"Try what?" she said, pretending not to know what he meant.

"Skinny dipping. There's no one around, so why not?"

She could think of many reasons why not, but she didn't say them. She only said: "Well, if you want to try it, go ahead."

He did go ahead. He dropped his swimsuit and flung it onto the towel that he had set on the beach, and then he bounded into the water.

Not for the first time she noticed he had a good body.

"Come on," he urged her, splashing around.

She didn't know what made her do it, but finally she unpeeled her one-piece swimsuit, folded it, and laid it neatly on her towel. She was in the water, up to her knees, when she finally felt the excitement of it: being naked, being in the water, being in the sun. And filled with joy, she joined Frank and splashed around, bobbing up and down in the clear water and feeling like she was being baptized, over and over.

Frank watched her, gazing at her in admiration. As she rose from the water reveling in her naked body he said: "You look like Venus in that painting of her rising from the sea."

"You mean by Botticelli?" she said, remembering the painting from an art history course at Fordham.

"Yeah, Botticelli."

"Well, I'm not a goddess or a movie star, but I'm somebody."

"Right. You're a Polish girl from Yonkers."

They came together and splashed around, enjoying the physical reality of each other, enjoying the touch of each other's skin, enjoying the water, enjoying the sun. It was like a rebirth, a readmission to life in the world, a joyous reaffirmation of love.

THE NEXT DAY they went to the hospital as soon as visitors were allowed, and when they arrived at the ICU the doctor was examining Jessica. They waited in the hall for a long time, and finally the doctor joined them and asked them to go into Jessica's room with him. The nurse was there, and Marika could tell from the expression on her face that things were going better. In fact, Jessica's eyes were open, and even though they seemed to be peering through a cloud she recognized them. She raised her arms and reached out for them, and they joined her in a three-way hug.

"Where am I?" Jessica asked.

"You're at St. John's," Marika said.

"What am I doing here?"

"We can talk about that later," Frank said. "Right now you gotta rest."

Meanwhile the doctor was giving instructions to the nurse, and then he asked them to go out into the hall with him.

"So how is she?" Marika asked him.

"She's better, but we'll have to keep her here for at least a few more days. You know, she's lucky to be alive."

"Well, I hope she feels lucky to be alive."

"I hope so too," the doctor said as if he cared.

"Can we go back and see her?"

"Yes, but don't stay longer than a half hour. Okay?"

"Okay." She thanked the doctor and led Frank back into their daughter's room, where they stayed longer than a half hour.

When they got home she called Nina and gave her the good news. Nina decided to leave work early and take a train that would arrive at Yonkers shortly after five, and Marika agreed to pick her up at the train station.

They had leftover pizza for lunch, sitting on the deck, and then while Frank went to his home office Marika went to their bedroom and lay down. Her mind got back on the rotary and eventually got off at a time when she was living in the city.

Tina finally met a guy she really liked. She asked him to join them for a drink after exercise class, and they met at the usual bar. The guy, whose name was Dennis, had rumpled blond air and perky blue eyes and an outgoing manner. He had grown up in Queens and gone to St. John's University, where he got a bachelor's in business administration. He had a job with a big insurance company settling claims, but he was looking for a job that would put him directly in contact with customers. He told a few stories that made them laugh and left them with a good impression.

After they had turned the corner onto 80th Street, while Frank continued walking up Second Avenue, Tina asked: "So what do you think of him?"

"I like him, and he made us laugh."

"Yeah, he has a great sense of humor."

"How did you meet him?"

"I was out with a girl I knew from City College having a drink when he appeared. He knew her, and they started talking, and I watched them talk. I could tell he wasn't her boyfriend, he was just her friend, and he made us laugh. He stayed after my girlfriend left, and we started talking, and we had another round of drinks, and well, you know."

Marika could imagine. "Does he live around here?"

"He lives on 76th Street near Second Avenue. He has a one-bedroom apartment. All to himself," Tina added.

Marika put an arm around Tina's waist, letting her know she was happy for her.

Now that Tina had a boyfriend Marika no longer felt guilty about leaving her alone at the apartment while she went out with Frank, and she started sleeping at his place on Saturday as well as Friday. They had stopped going to Yonkers on Saturdays, so they only had to get up on Sunday morning, have breakfast, shower, dress, and take a subway from 86th Street to Woodlawn, where their fathers were waiting for them.

After being with Frank for a whole week in Tortola without interruptions for work or family she knew she wanted to live with him, and one Saturday morning as they were lying in bed, deferring the process of getting up, she broached the subject by saying: "You know, when I came back to my apartment after our trip I missed being with you."

"I missed being with you," he said.

"So maybe we should be with each other more."

"Yeah. Would you like to move in with me?"

"I would," she said. "But I don't think I should unless we're engaged."

"Then let's get engaged."

"You really want to get engaged?" she asked, rolling toward him and searching his face.

"I really do," he assured her.

Feeling that it was the right thing to do, she said: "So let's get engaged."

They sealed the agreement with a long kiss.

"What kind of ring would you like?"

"I don't know. Are engagement rings always diamonds?"

"Not always. They can be whatever stone you like."

"Are emeralds more expensive than diamonds?"

"I have no idea, but if you want an emerald it doesn't matter. I mean within reason."

"I don't want an expensive ring," she assured him. "I only want a beautiful ring."

"Then let's go and look at rings."

Having a purpose for getting up, she got out of bed and took a shower and dressed in the casual weekend clothes that she had brought with her in a tote bag. Her work clothes were neatly folded in a drawer and hanging in the closet.

After a breakfast of coffee with pastries from the local bakery they left the apartment and went down the stairs. She could see how living in a five-floor walkup would prevent you from forgetting something and having to go back up to get it.

They were wearing winter coats and gloves because it was still

February, which though it was short on the calendar always seemed long because of the weather. It was cold, but it was a clear sunny day, so instead of taking a bus across 79th Street they walked all the way to Fifth Avenue and then headed downtown, looking for jewelry stores. Of course they stopped at Tiffany's but Marika felt uncomfortable there with all those snooty sales people and pretentious customers, so after looking at a few expensive rings, which she didn't like, they moved on.

After a while they came to a small store that dealt in antique jewelry, where they were waited on by the owner and treated with respect. When she mentioned the possibility of an emerald the man reached down into the display case and brought out a ring with small emeralds halfway around it, accompanied by even smaller diamonds. As she tried it on her finger he explained the ring was a recent acquisition from an estate sale in England, and he pointed out the initials and date engraved inside the band.

She looked at Frank, and she knew he could tell from her eyes that she hoped this ring wasn't too expensive because she loved it. Actually, it was a lot less than the rings they had seen at Tiffany's, so Frank took out his checkbook and paid for it, having noticed a sign that said the store preferred checks to credit cards. The owner asked her for the ring so he could clean it, and then he put it into a pouch and into a box with the store's name on it.

She kept the box in her pocketbook until they got back to Frank's apartment, and there he took the ring out and put it on her finger.

Filled with joy, she said: "We're engaged."

"Yeah," he said. "I'm your fiancé."

"And I'm your fiancée."

They kissed, and that eventually led them back to bed for the rest of the morning.

The next morning before they went to church she told her parents the news. She had held back from telling her father in the car after he had picked her up at Woodlawn because she wanted to tell them both at the same time. They were sitting at the kitchen table having coffee.

"Look," she said, showing them her left hand with the ring on her fourth finger. "Frank and I have gotten engaged."

"That's wonderful!" her mother said. "What a beautiful ring."

"We found it at a jewelry store on Madison Avenue. It's from England, and it's an antique."

"When did Frank give it for you?"

"Yesterday. We decided it was time to get engaged."

"Did Frank get down on his knees and propose to you?' her father asked her jokingly.

"No, not exactly," she said, recalling how it had happened in bed. "But he did propose, and I accepted."

"He's a lucky guy," her father said.

"I'm a lucky girl," she said.

"God bless you both," her mother said. "When do you plan to have the wedding?"

"Well, we're thinking about late September or early October."

"I think early October would be better. It would give you more time for the preparations."

"Okay," she said, deferring to her mother.

"Are you planning to have the wedding at St. Casimir?"

"Yeah, I think so. I was baptized and confirmed there. But we could have it at St. Brigid. What do you think?"

"I think the people from our side would prefer St. Casimir, though I don't know about the people from Frank's side."

"From what he's told me," Marika said, "they mostly live in the area where he grew up, so St. Casimir would be closer for them."

"Then you should have the wedding at St. Casimir."

"Okay. And we should have the reception at the Polish Center."

"That would make sense," her mother said.

"We had our reception at the Polish Center," her father said.

"Remember? We had such a good time."

With that settled they talked about scheduling. Her father pointed out that the Polish Center was booked for events way ahead of time, so they should find possible dates for the reception first and then talk to the priest and see if any of those dates was available for the wedding. Her mother suggested that she come to Yonkers next Saturday for that purpose.

After Mass they went to the Chart House for brunch, and while they were eating they talked more about the wedding.

"I assume that Julia will be your maid of honor," her mother said as if it was a done deal.

"Of course," she said, though she would have preferred Tina for that role because as usual her sister would want to be the center of attention.

"If she's the maid of honor," her father said wryly, "she'll have to wear a dress."

"We'll pick out the dress for her," her mother assured him. "She'll only have to go with us and try it on."

"I can't remember the last time I saw her in a dress."

"She wore a dress for confirmation."

"How long ago was that? Twenty years ago?"

"It was seventeen years ago."

"So I was close. Well, it'll be good to see her in a dress."

"Speaking of dresses," her mother said. "We have to get a wedding dress."

"Well, I don't want you to spend a lot of money," Marika said. "When I hear what girls are spending on their wedding dresses, I just can't believe it."

"Don't worry," her mother said. "We'll find a beautiful dress for you."

"A beautiful dress for a beautiful bride," her father said, raising his glass of Bloody Mary and toasting her with it.

Since she had to ask Julia to be her maid of honor she called her and arranged to meet her for dinner a few nights later. It took them a while to agree on a place because Julia didn't want to come to the Upper East Side and Marika didn't want to go down to Tribeca, so they met at a restaurant in Murray Hill, which they could both easily get to from their offices. They hadn't seen each other since the last time they had both gone to visit their parents, and that was several months ago. They had agreed to meet at six o'clock, and Marika arrived on time, but she had to wait a half hour for Julia, who apologized and explained that she was working on a deal that would make millions for her firm.

Marika was already sipping a white wine, and after getting the waiter's attention Julia ordered a red wine and then asked: "So what's new?"

"Frank and I are getting married."

"Frank? You mean the guy you met in exercise class?"

"Yeah. We've been dating for a year and a half."

"That's not very long. Are you sure he's the right guy for you?"

"Yeah, I'm sure," she said. "We're going to have the wedding in early October."

At that point the waiter set a glass of wine in front of Julia, who reached for it and took a drink, tasting the wine as if she was a connoisseur.

"I want you be my maid of honor," Marika told her.

With her mouth still full of wine Julia shook her head, and then after swallowing it she said: "You don't need a maid of honor. In fact, you don't need a traditional wedding."

"I don't need one, but our parents expect one."

"So you're doing it to make them happy?"

"Yeah. I owe it to them after all they've done for me."

"Well, I hope you're not getting married to please them."

"I'm not. I'm getting married because I love Frank and I want to spend my life with him."

Julia made a face of disgust. "You know, you don't have to marry the guy. You could just live with him."

"I don't want to just live with him," she said. "I want to be married to him."

"Okay. If that's what you want, then go ahead. But you can marry him without having a traditional wedding."

"I told you," she said patiently, "our parents expect a traditional wedding. And I don't have a problem with it."

"But you don't need a maid of honor."

"I know I don't need one, but I want to have one."

"Then ask your roommate," Julia said, "whatever her name is."

She refrained from saying that she would have preferred her roommate all along. Instead, she said: "Mom expects you to be my maid of honor."

"If she does, she can tell me directly."

"Okay. I'll ask her to call you."

At that point she dropped the subject of the wedding, and Julia picked up the subject of an ingenious deal that would make millions for her firm.

When she got home she called her mother and asked her to call Julia, explaining why. She almost hoped that her mother wouldn't succeed in bringing Julia around so she could ask Tina to be her maid of honor. But the next day she heard from her mother, who told her that Julia had agreed to be the maid of honor, and she was glad to have the matter resolved.

Now that she and Frank were engaged she felt it would be all right for her to move in with him, though she knew her parents wouldn't approve, so she didn't tell them about it. Also, she did it gradually, taking a bag of her things every time she went to his apartment, and by the end of June she was settled there. Of course seeing him every day, eating breakfast and dinner with him every day, and sleeping with him every night was different from seeing him two or three times a week, so she had to adapt.

One thing different was food shopping, which they mainly did together now, buying staples as well as specific items they needed for the meals they planned. They had many sources of food in the neighborhood, including a Hungarian butcher shop, an Italian fish store, a German bakery, a Korean vegetable store, plus the supermarket on York Avenue. They tried cooking dinner together, but they got in each other's way, so from then on only one of them cooked at a time, and they both cleaned up.

They usually went out for dinner on Friday. They only had to walk a few blocks to restaurants that included Italian, Spanish, German, Hungarian, and Czech. And during June they discovered a new French restaurant on 83rd Street between First and York

Avenues that became their favorite. Frank especially liked their chicken with wine vinegar, and Marika liked their filet of sole in tarragon sauce.

Though they lived together, they continued going to their parents' houses separately, and on a Saturday in early March her father drove her and her mother to the Polish Center to get possible dates for the reception, then to St. Casimir to set a date for the wedding, and then to stores in White Plains and Eastchester to look for a wedding dress. Her mother, who had saved money from her salary at the phone company to pay for the wedding dress, urged her to buy whatever she wanted and not to worry about the price, but having been conditioned by her parents to be frugal Marika wanted to find a dress that was not only beautiful but also affordable.

That evening Marika and Frank had dinner with both sets of their parents to celebrate their engagement. They went to the restaurant on Bronx River Road where they had gone before. When they had ordered food Frank's father had the waiter bring a bottle of prosecco for a toast, and as they raised their glasses he said with emotion: "God bless Marika and Franco. God bless them now, and God bless them throughout their lives."

In the meantime Tina had lined up a new roommate, a girl she knew from City College. Since Marika no longer lived in the apartment she told Tina it was all right for this girl to move in with her, and in return they arranged for Tina to cover for her if her mother called her at the apartment. Tina would tell her mother she was doing laundry or some other chore, would take a message from her mother, and then would call her at Frank's apartment so she could call her mother back. But luckily that didn't happen very often or else her mother would begin to wonder why Marika was always unavailable when she called her.

By the time October came around Marika and Frank had made the adjustments of living together, and they were ready for the wedding. The church was filled with people from both sides of their families, and walking up the aisle on her father's arm Marika gave thanks for being blessed with her family and Frank, who was waiting for her near the altar with the priest, his younger brother, and Julia. He bowed respectfully as her father handed her over to him, and they stood next to each other as the priest began the wedding Mass: "In the name of the Father, and of the Son, and of the Holy Spirit."

"Amen," Marika said after crossing herself. She committed herself to every word of the ceremony, and during the exchange of vows with Frank she was deeply conscious of the fact that marriage was a sacrament.

Though the Polish Center was only a short distance away, a limousine took them there from the church. They stopped for a while in an anteroom to have pictures taken before going into the room where the reception was being held. At the entrance they were greeted by both sets of parents. Her father, with her mother standing next to him, was holding a tray on which there was a plate of bread, a glass of wine, and salt. He began the ceremony by saying: "*Zgodnie z naszą staropolską tradycją witamy Cię chlebem, winem i solą, aby Twój dom zawsze cieszył się obfitością.*"

Marika translated for Frank and his parents: "According to our old Polish tradition, we greet you with bread, wine, and salt so your home might always enjoy abundance."

"What a nice tradition," Frank's mother said.

"It's a blessing from our parents," she explained. "The bread is given in the hope that we never go hungry. The wine in the hope that we never go thirsty. And overall that our lives be filled with health and happiness."

"Thank you," Frank and his parents said.

"Oh, and the salt is to remind us that life may be difficult at times, and that we must learn to cope with those situations."

"Well, let's hope we don't have too much salt."

She took a piece of bread and a sip of wine, and Frank did likewise. She knew that according to the tradition they were supposed to break the plate and the glass, but she didn't want to make a mess for someone to clean up, so she skipped that part of the ceremony.

Stepping forward onto the floor, which in the middle of the

tables had been cleared for dancing, they were welcomed by applause from their guests, and with the band playing the song they had requested they did the first dance. It was a song that had been released a few months ago and was being played all the time on the radio: "I Just Called to Say I Love You." It was easy to dance to, and Frank led her gracefully around the floor.

Later, before dessert was served, her father got the band to play a polka, and he asked her to dance. She loved dancing the polka with him, and they were cheered as they whirled around and then joined by couples from her side of the family. The band, which had been hired by the Polish Center, had a large repertoire of polkas, and they played one polka after another until it was time to serve dessert. The man who organized the reception had urged her to have cherries jubilee, which they would serve theatrically on flaming skewers, but Marika hadn't liked that idea and instead had requested kremówka, a cake with vanilla cream between layers of puff pastry.

At the end Marika performed the ritual of throwing her bouquet to the single girls. She aimed the bouquet at her sister, meaning well, but Julia tipped it right into the hands of Tina, who smiled with joy at her good fortune. Along with Tina and Evelyn, her friends from Fordham had attended the wedding, and Marika gave hugs to all of them before she got into the car that Frank had rented for their honeymoon.

They were going to an inn in Mystic, Connecticut, which a colleague of Frank had recommended. It was only about a two-hour drive from Yonkers, and they got there by eight. The inn was an old rambling structure, built of wood and painted white like most of the houses in New England. Their room was on the second floor, and the inn didn't have an elevator, but since they were in good shape from living in a five-floor walkup it didn't bother them to walk up two flights of stairs with luggage. The room was a suite with a view down the main street of town to a drawbridge that spanned the river. By then Marika was so exhausted and the queen size bed was so alluring that she felt like lying down in her clothes on top of the bedspread and calling it a night, but it was too early to go to bed, so they went down to the bar, which was in an Italian restaurant that occupied most of the main floor of the building. They asked the bartender for a menu, which they perused, and they decided to have dinner there the next day.

It was almost ten when they got to bed, and as they faced each other with heads on the pillows Marika said: "So I'm not Marika Janczewski anymore, I'm Marika Bonetti."

"Do you like the change?"

"Yeah, I like it. At least it'll be easier for people to pronounce."

"Well, I've had people mispronounce it," Frank said. "When I was doing basic training in South Carolina the sergeants couldn't pronounce any last names that ended in a vowel."

"So what did they call you?"

"Bonnet," he said.

"That doesn't sound like a guy's name."

"It wasn't supposed to. It was a way of harassing me."

"Oh, yeah, I get it. So did you ever think of yourself as Frank Bonnet?"

"No, I never did. But I learned how to respond to that name. I had no choice."

"Well, I know what that's like," she said. "I've been in situations where I had no choice."

"Like what?" he asked.

"Like having to share a room with my sister."

"Yeah, I noticed how she avoided catching your bouquet."

"She didn't want to catch the bouquet because it came from me. She never liked getting hand-me-downs from me."

"My brother was that way. But he had no choice. We didn't have a lot of money."

"We didn't either, so she had no choice. But she still didn't like getting hand-me-downs. Instead, she destroyed them." She remembered the dolls she had happily played with and the clothes she had taken such good care of, dismembered and torn by Julia after they were handed down to her, and it made her sad.

"Then maybe it's a good thing she didn't catch your bouquet."

"Yeah." She imagined her sister destroying the flowers. But then she chided herself for having such a thought on a day when she had been so blessed. And she erased it by telling Frank: "I love you."

"I love you too."

They slept well, and after breakfast the next morning they went for a walk on the main street of town, crossing the drawbridge, pausing to look in the windows of stores and to read the menus of restaurants. There was a variety of stores, including high-end clothing stores, accessory stores, an army-navy store, an ice cream store, a candy store, a print store, and two gift stores, but her favorite was the bookstore, where they spent more than an hour with Marika scanning recent novels and Frank searching the cooking section until he found what he was looking for—a Polish cookbook. To plan their dinners during the week they made a schedule with each of them assigned specific dishes. Frank did Italian dishes, usually pastas, and she did chicken and fish dishes, but never Polish because her family only had Polish food on holidays, birthdays, or other special occasions, which her mother prepared, so they really didn't need a Polish cookbook. But Frank wanted to learn how to make pierogi and gołąbki and kapusta, so she didn't talk him out of buying the cookbook. For herself she bought two current novels, and then they kept walking until they came to the art center. By then it was almost time for lunch, so they deferred a visit to the art center and walked back to the inn, where they left their purchases and got into the car to drive to Stonington.

The colleague of Frank who had recommended Mystic had also told him about a restaurant that was out on a pier in Stonington Harbor, so they had decided to have lunch there. It took them less than twenty minutes to get there, and since the weather was still warm enough to sit outside they got a table on the pier overlooking the harbor. The view of the harbor, with boats at anchor in the shimmering water, made them speculate about the possibility of living in Stonington, though of course it was an idle dream. For lunch they had lobster rolls, Connecticut style, with warm butter in a brioche. It was Marika's first lobster roll, and she liked it so much that she resolved to find a restaurant in the city that served lobster rolls.

Back at the inn they lounged in bed for a while, and then they went to the art center, which had an exhibition of local artists. The paintings were mostly of landscapes and seascapes, but one in particular got their attention: a painting of the restaurant in Stonington Harbor were they had eaten lunch. They both liked it, and feeling they were fated to buy it they asked the woman who had welcomed them how much it was. Though its price was higher than they had expected, they went ahead and bought it to hang on a wall and remind them of their honeymoon.

EIGHT

THAT AFTERNOON THEY drove to the hospital in Marika's car so she could leave and pick up Nina at the train station. They found Jessica sitting up in bed, with lines still hooked up to her but looking better. There was a tinge of rose in her cheeks.

After some introductory talk Jessica asked: "When will they let me out of here?"

"When you're all right," Marika told her.

"Well, I feel fine."

"That's good," Frank said. "So just let them take care of you, and you'll feel even better."

Jessica closed her eyes for a while, and then she asked: "What happened to me?"

Not being sure about what the doctor or the nurse had told her, Marika said: "You took an overdose of a drug."

"I did? I don't remember doing that."

"I'm sure you didn't do it deliberately, but do you remember who you were with?"

After a moment Jessica said: "I was with a girl I met on the internet. I went to her apartment, and we had a drink. But that's the last thing I remember."

"Did you do things with her before?" Frank asked.

"No, I just met her. She gave me the address of her apartment, and I drove there." A pause. "What happened to my car?"

"We went there and got it and brought it home."

"Did you see the girl?"

"We didn't see anyone. The place was abandoned. No one was living there."

Jessica frowned. "What was the drug?"

"It was fentanyl," Marika said.

"Fentanyl? That's bad shit."

"It's really bad shit, and it almost killed you."

"Oh, my God." Jessica started crying. "I'm sorry, I'm sorry."

"It's all right," Frank said. "What matters is that it didn't kill you. And maybe you'll learn from this experience."

They stayed with Jessica until the nurse made them leave, and then they went to the waiting area, where there were other people so they couldn't talk. At four-thirty Marika left to go to the train station, and Frank waited, checking messages on his phone.

Marika parked her car on the street and waited standing in front of the station. An announcement over a loudspeaker said that the train was late, so she wandered into the little park where there was a statue of Ella Fitzgerald, a native of Yonkers, and she sat down on a bench. She gazed up into the trees, remembering happy times from the past.

After their wedding Marika enjoyed a period of marital bliss. She loved Frank, and he loved her. They got along fine, they didn't have fights, they didn't even have arguments, though at times they had discussions that led to agreements that were compromises between their two positions. They did have personality differences which increased their appreciation of each other. They were both organized, and they were both orderly, but she wanted things in perfect order, whereas Frank only wanted them in good enough order, and he would sometimes joke about her need for perfection, which she maintained was only a desire and not a need. For example, they had a teapot with a whistle on the spout, and when you wanted to pour boiling water out of the teapot into a coffee filter or cup, you had to open the cap of the spout. Marika always closed the cap after using it, but Frank didn't always close it, and if she saw the cap still open it drove her crazy. So once Frank deliberately left the cap open just to see how she would react, and when she compulsively closed the cap he hugged her, saying: "I love you."

"I love you too, but you know it drives me crazy when you leave that cap open, so why did you do it?"

"I did it to see you being you."

"What do you mean?"

"I love what you are, not what you or anyone else believes you should be."

She had to think about that for a moment before she understood it. "Then you don't mind if I sometimes act like an obsessive-compulsive nut?"

"No, I don't mind. I appreciate it. And I bet when you edit a book you don't miss a single error that your authors make."

"I try not to, but sometimes I miss things."

"So you're not a perfectionist, which is good. You just want things to be as good as you can make them."

She could see that Frank really understood her. Not that she had ever felt misunderstood by other people, but still it felt good to have this kind of validation, especially from him.

The thing that occasionally bothered her about him was his very strong commitment to his work. She never doubted that if he had to choose between her and his work he would choose her, but there were times when he stayed late at his office to finish something, rather than stop and let it rest until the next day. And he agreed to work on this problem.

Of course their marriage wasn't only about them, it was also about their families, and they worked out how to spend time with their parents. They alternated between their parents on Sundays, taking the subway to Woodlawn and going to Mass at St. Brigid with her parents or Mass at St. Frances with his parents. They had Thanksgiving dinner with both families at his parents' house. They had the Wigilia supper on Christmas Eve with her family and went to midnight Mass at St. Casimir, agreeing to have the Feast of Seven Fishes with his family the next year. And they had Christmas dinner with both families at his parents' house.

In January her father called her at work and told her Ciocia Anna had passed away. She was shocked by the loss, and she felt it keenly because Ciocia Anna had been like a grandmother to her. But she knew it was a much greater loss for her mother because Ciocia Anna had been like a mother to her, so while she was still on the phone with her father she checked the train schedule and told him she would be on the 1:20 train to Yonkers. At her father's request she called Julia to give her the news, but Julia was in a meeting, so she left a message for her.

Her father picked her up at the Yonkers station and drove her home. When she saw her mother stricken with grief she was glad she had come right away, and she did her best to console her mother, imagining how she would feel if she lost her mother. She spent the night in her old room, and she took several days off work to help with the wake and the funeral. Frank was by her side for both events, but Julia only made it to the funeral at the last minute.

A few weeks later she had to deal with the rumor that a gigantic publishing company had made an offer for her company with the intention of merging her company with theirs and eliminating a lot of positions. She lived with the threat of losing her job until the end of April, but eventually the takeover didn't happen because the family that owned her company got its act together and refused the offer.

By then she and Frank both felt they needed a vacation, so he did some research and found a deal at a resort in Puerto Plata, Dominican Republic. Since the price included the hotel and meals and the round-trip flight they could afford it, and since they didn't have to take a second flight on a small plane they booked the trip for the middle of May.

As they drove from the airport to the hotel she could see that this was a different country from Tortola. The signs were all in Spanish, and the cars were greatly outnumbered by motorbikes which swerved around them with one, two, three, and even four people on them as well as furniture and propane tanks. Their driver astutely avoided the bikes and got them safely to the hotel, a Spanish-style low-rise building surrounded by palm trees.

As soon as they were settled in their room they changed into their swimsuits and headed to the beach. The water was the same turquoise color that she remembered from Tortola, and the sand was fine and soft and warm under her toes. It was a lovely beach, but it wasn't deserted, so they couldn't even think about skinny dipping.

The hotel belonged to a Spanish chain, and for dinner Marika had her first paella, which she liked as much as her first lobster roll. They danced for a while after dinner in the open-air lounge where a band was playing Latin music, and then they headed for their room, where they found two gold-wrapped chocolates on the bed. Later, when they said goodnight they agreed that it was like having a second honeymoon.

After a few days of having all their meals at the hotel they followed the recommendation of a woman that Marika had befriended on the beach, and they took a cab to Santa Cruz, a town about fifteen miles west of Puerto Plata. The road going into the town was bumpy, and they passed a poor neighborhood of diversely painted wooden houses with metal roofs which gave Marika a feeling of guilt for being what the people who lived there probably saw as a rich American tourist, and though the feeling didn't completely go away, her spirits were raised by the sight of the beach, a crescent of sand that reminded her of Long Bay.

The driver took them to a restaurant that was right on the beach, and they sat at a table in the shade of a large green umbrella that promoted a beer called Presidente. A pretty young woman gave them menus and took their order for two Presidentes, which was ice cold and tasted like it was made for the beach. Frank ordered chivo, which meant goat, and she ordered pescado frito, which meant fried fish. Their plates came with mounds of white rice and bowls of soupy pink beans, which they mixed with the rice. It was their first meal of real Dominican food, and they enjoyed it so much that they resolved to find a Dominican restaurant back home.

That lunch on the beach was one of the high points of their vacation. The only low point occurred the next day when they were sitting in lounge chairs at the edge of the beach in front of their hotel. A pair of big white men walked by them, speaking Russian. She could understand most of what they said, and it wasn't nice. They had checked her out and they were speculating about what it would be like to have sex with her. If they had just been guys making remarks about her she wouldn't have minded because she was used to it, but the fact that they were Russians talking about her that way pierced her in a vulnerable spot.

"Are you all right?" Frank asked.

"Yeah," she said, reaching for his hand.

"Did those guys say something that bothered you?"

"It wasn't what they said, it was who they were."

"Okay. Who were they?"

"They were Russians," she said as if that explained everything.

"So you could understand them?"

"Not every word, but I got most of it."

"What did they say?"

"They were speculating about what it would be like to have sex with me."

Frank moved as if he intended to go after them.

"No, don't do anything. I'm used to guys making remarks about me. What bothered me was that they were Russians."

After a moment Frank said: "I think I understand. I mean, I've heard the way your parents talk about Russians."

"My parents have reasons for hating Russians. They raped and killed my mother's sister, and they killed my father's mother. They made our country their colony."

"I understand. Well, they won't control Poland forever."

"Oh, I don't know," she said, not sharing his optimism. "Whenever there's resistance they crush it."

Frank was silent for a while, and then he said: "Whenever there was resistance to the government of South Vietnam they crushed it. And look what happened to them. They even had us fighting for them, and they still lost."

"Why did they lose?"

"They were on the wrong side," Frank told her. "And from what I know about it, the Russians are on the wrong side in Poland."

She was glad to hear Frank say this, and she wished her parents could have heard him say it because she knew their hearts were still in Poland. In appreciation she leaned over and kissed her husband tenderly.

During that summer everything went well not only with their marriage but also with their jobs. She was assigned some good books to edit, and Frank was assigned some good projects to work on. And they had a good social life, which on her side involved her friends from Fordham and their husbands as well as Tina and her boyfriend and on Frank's side involved his friends from Manhattan College and their wives as well as some guys who had served in the marines with him. On an impulse they decided to have a party, and all those people came and stayed until the early hours of the morning. So it was a summer that she would happily remember.

On Labor Day they drove her parents to Frank's parents' house for a cookout. Her mother looked well and even had a glass of sambuca after dinner, so Marika was stunned when her father called her the next day early in the morning, before she had gotten out of bed, and told her that her mother was gone. At first she didn't understand because she couldn't imagine where her mother might have gone, but then she realized that her father meant her mother had died. He told her how he had found her beside him in bed, lifeless, and how he had called 911 in case they could revive her, but it was too late, and they had taken her to St. John's Hospital in order to determine the cause of death. He was waiting to hear from the hospital.

After telling him she would be in Yonkers as soon as possible she called her sister, who was at her apartment having breakfast. Julia's first reaction was to shriek and deny what had happened, but after carrying on for a while she got herself under control enough so they could agree on when to meet at Grand Central for a train to Yonkers.

Marika and Frank quickly dressed and left the apartment and walked to York Avenue where they found a taxi. Though it was early rush hour it didn't take them long to get to Grand Central. They bought tickets and waited at the information center for Julia, who arrived about twenty minutes later. Julia was hysterical, but with Frank's help Marika calmed her down enough to get her on the train. On the ride to Yonkers, which seemed to take twice as long as usual, Julia kept saying: "Mommy was everything to me, and now I have nothing. Now I have nothing."

Marika, sitting across from her sister, held her hands and did what she could to comfort her, but she was barely able to hold herself together, and if Frank hadn't been there with her she might have fallen apart like her sister.

At the Yonkers station they got a taxi that took them to their parents' house. When their father opened the door for them and Marika saw tears in his eyes, which she had never seen before, her heart went out to him, and she put her arms around him and held him tight, being comforted as well as comforting.

Behind her Julia was emoting again, and Frank was trying to calm her down, so Marika let go of her father and turned toward Julia who instead of going into their father's arms confronted him by asking: "What happened to Mommy?"

"They say she had a heart attack," their father said.

"But she didn't have a heart problem," Julia said.

"They say it could have been congenital. Her mother also died of a heart attack."

"Well, her doctor should have diagnosed the problem."

"She had regular checkups, and as far as her doctor could tell she was fine."

"Then she should have had a better doctor."

Refusing to pursue the conversation, their father said: "I made coffee for you."

So they went into the kitchen, where Marika poured mugs of coffee for Frank and herself, with Julia declining, and they sat down at the kitchen table.

"Where is she now?" Julia asked.

"She's still at the hospital," their father said, "but they'll move her to the funeral home."

"Which funeral home?"

"The one we used for Uncle Walter and Ciocia Anna."

"Where is it?"

"On Yonkers Avenue," Marika said. It was the funeral home

that had served the Polish community for generations. "You've been there."

"Well, I want to see her," Julia said as if she didn't trust what she had been told.

"You can see her after they prepare her," Marika said, taking charge. "We'll have an open casket as usual."

After a silence their father said: "I made an appointment to meet with the funeral director tomorrow morning."

"I'll go with you," Marika said.

"I'll go too," Julia said. "I want to see her."

"They probably won't have her ready by tomorrow," Marika said, based on her experience with the funerals of Uncle Walter and Ciocia Anna.

"You can see her at the wake," their father told Julia.

After stewing at the table for a while Julia left them and went upstairs to her room.

Marika and Frank took advantage of the silence to call their offices and say they wouldn't be coming in that day because of a death in the family. They sat in the kitchen for the rest of the morning, not talking much but just being with each other. Around noon Frank went out and got sandwiches at the food store on Palisade Avenue, and while he was gone Marika went upstairs to check on her sister. She found Julia lying on her bed.

"Are you all right?" she asked gently.

"No, I'm not all right. I lost Mommy, and now I have nothing."

"Well, Dad lost her too. Have you thought about how he must feel?"

"He still has you," Julia said.

"He also has you. And we're something," Marika said, "but Mom was his life, and they were married for more than thirty years."

Julia was silent for a while, and then she said: "It's not fair. I mean, I'm too young to lose my mother."

Marika could have pointed out that their mother had lost her mother at the age of twenty, but instead she reached down and patted Julia on the shoulder and left the room, feeling the loss for all of them but mostly for her father.

The next morning Marika and her father went to the funeral home without Julia, who stayed in bed. The director, a woman around her mother's age, greeted them saying: *"Bardzo mi przykro z powodu twojej straty."*

"Dziękuję," her father said.

"Your mother was a courageous person," the woman told Marika continuing in Polish. "She came here as an orphan and became a valued member of our community."

"I know," Marika said with tears forming in her eyes.

"We'll all miss her, but of course your family will miss her most, so we'll pray for you."

"Dziękuję," Marika said.

"It's a great loss for you and for our community, but it's a comfort to know that Bozena is in heaven now with the Blessed Mother and all the angels. God bless her soul."

"Boże pobłogosław jej duszę," Marika said softly.

After some further conversation they got down to the business of choosing the casket and discussing possible dates for the funeral Mass and the burial that would be arranged between the funeral home and the priest. Since today was Wednesday it was possible to have the funeral on Saturday, but it was also possible to have it on Tuesday of the following week. Marika was going to let her father make the decision, and though he said he preferred to have the funeral on Saturday, he didn't take a firm stand, which wasn't like him, and sensing that his mind was clouded by grief she made the decision to have the funeral on Saturday, which meant that the viewing would be on Friday.

As they left the funeral home and started walking toward the car her father put an arm around her shoulder and said: *"Dziękuję. That wasn't easy."*

"To nie było łatwe," she agreed, putting an arm around his waist.

"Jesteś teraz główną panią," he said, which meant: "You're the head lady now."

She already knew that, but her father had just made it official. And looking ahead, she saw the responsibilities she would have to assume.

Her father stood at the head of the reception line at the first session of the viewing, she stood next to her father, Julia stood next to her, and then Frank, who helped to support Julia. It was an ordeal, but she was impressed by the number of people who came to express their condolences. There were people from their old and new neighborhoods, members of both St. Casimir and St. Brigid churches, colleagues from the phone company, and friends of Uncle Walter and Ciocia Anna. At the second session Frank's parents arrived, bringing their younger son with them, and Marika thanked them especially for coming.

When the second session finally ended with prayers by a priest who had recently arrived from Poland, she was wiped out, and she had to fight fatigue to stay up with her father and Frank in the living room for a shot of vodka after Julia had gone to bed. The vodka was rough but once it went down she could feel the tension in her body subsiding, and it helped even more when Frank massaged her shoulders in her room. As they had been doing since Tuesday night they slept in the twin beds that she and Julia had used after Ciocia Anna moved in following the death of Uncle Walter. They had tried sleeping together in one of the beds, but as much as they liked being next to each other there just wasn't enough room for both of them.

For the funeral she wore the navy blue dress that she had bought for Ciocia Anna's funeral, and again she was impressed by the number of people who attended. She remembered the funeral director saying that her mother had been a valued member of the community, and the sight of all those people in the church confirmed this statement. It made Marika feel lucky to be her mother's daughter. Her family sat together in the front pew on the left, with her father next to the aisle, and then Marika, Julia, and Frank. She turned and faced the aisle as the casket was carried by men from the funeral home, knowing she had to hold herself together and support the others because she was now, as her father had told her, the head lady.

They followed the order of the Mass, and when it was time for her do to the first reading (Julia had pleaded out of a second, optional reading) she walked up to the podium and faced the congregation and read: "A reading from the first Letter of Saint Paul to the Thessalonians. We do not want you to be unaware, brothers and sisters, about those who have fallen asleep, so that you may not grieve like the rest, who have no hope. For if we believe that Jesus died and rose, so too will God, through Jesus, bring with him those who have fallen asleep. Indeed, we tell you this, on the word of the Lord, that we who are alive, who are left until the coming of the Lord, will surely not precede those who have fallen asleep. For the Lord himself, with a word of command, with the voice of an archangel and with the trumpet of God, will come down from heaven, and the dead in Christ will rise first. Then we who are alive, who are left, will be caught up together with them in the clouds to meet the Lord in the air. Thus we shall always be with the Lord. Therefore, console one another with these words. The Word of the Lord." She descended carefully and returned to their pew, where her father patted her on the shoulder to let her know she had done a good job.

The burial was at St. Joseph's Cemetery in the plot that Uncle Walter and Ciocia Anna had bought for their family. As she watched the casket being lowered into the grave Marika said a prayer of thanks for her mother.

There was a funeral lunch at the Polish Center, but Julia begged off, so they left her at the house before heading downtown again. At her father's request Frank drove them there and parked in the lot, which was almost filled with cars. The funeral home had rented a room and engaged a cook to prepare a feast of Polish food, and people were already seated at tables, eating pierogi, gołąbki, kielbasa, and kapusta with glasses of beer. They joined some people from St. Casimir who were sitting at a table with empty chairs, and after talking with them for a while Marika realized that she was hungry, so she got up and asked her father if she could get him anything, and he said yes, she could get him a beer. Frank went with her to the serving table, and while he filled their plates with food she took a glass of beer to her father.

Frank loved the food, and with her encouragement he went into the kitchen and returned with the cook's recipe for kapusta, which he said he would make for the next family holiday. By then Marika was feeling better thanks to several glasses of wine, but she still wondered if without her mother they would have another family holiday.

When they got home she checked to see how Julia was, and she found her sister lying in bed, not sleeping but just lying there, staring at the ceiling.

"I brought you a plate of food," she told Julia. "I left it in the kitchen for you."

"Thanks anyway. I don't want it."

"But you must be hungry. You haven't eaten anything since breakfast."

"The last thing I need is a Jewish mother. So why don't you just leave me alone."

"Okay," Marika said, hurt by her sister's rudeness. But she mitigated the pain by reminding herself that Julia had never been good at dealing with adversity.

The next afternoon they took the train back to the city. They left Julia at Grand Central, where she was going to take the shuttle to Times Square, and they took the Lexington subway up to 86th Street. She didn't mind climbing up the stairs to their apartment because she was so glad to be home and be able to sleep in the same bed with Frank.

During that week she called her father several times to see how he was doing, and from what she heard over the phone she didn't think he was doing well, so on Saturday afternoon she and Frank took the train to Yonkers and a taxi to her father's house. Though he was expecting them they found him in the living room in his undershirt watching a football game on television and drinking shots out of a bottle of Wyborowa. He had also been smoking cigars in the house, which her mother had never allowed. The air was thick with the smell of cigar smoke, which she had never minded because it was associated with her father, but his violation of her mother's rule struck her as a sign of dissolution. At that point she knew she had to live closer to him so she could make sure he was all right.

Since he wasn't in any condition to go out for dinner as they had planned, Frank made pasta with things he found in the cabinet, which they ate at the dining room table. Her father didn't say much during dinner, and instead of having an after-dinner drink with them he apologized for not being better company and went up to bed.

"I'm worried about him," Marika said as she and Frank settled on the sofa in the living room after doing the dishes and cleaning up.

"I am too," Frank said.

"I mean, he's lost without my mother."

"It must be very hard for him."

"And I don't want to see him go downhill."

"I don't think he will. He's a very strong man.

"I know," she said, "but he depended on my mother for his social life, and without her I worry about him being alone."

"Well, he knows a lot of people in the community."

"He does, but my mother was the one who got him to do things outside the family."

After a pause Frank said: "I guess it's the same with my father. My mother's the one who gets him to do things outside the family."

"So you understand. And now I feel responsible for him."

"But you can't do what your mother did for him."

"I know I can't, but I have to do something."

"What are you thinking?"

"I'm thinking we should move to Yonkers so we can be closer to him."

"You think we should move into this house and live with him?"

"No. I think we should have our own house, but I want to be closer to him. And anyway,' she added, "he wouldn't want us to live with him."

"I guess he wouldn't," Frank said.

"So we should start looking for a house."

"Okay. We have two incomes, so we can afford to pay a mortgage. And if we live in a house," he added, "you won't have to climb up five flights of stairs."

She picked up a cushion and threw it at him playfully, saying: "You weren't supposed to guess my ulterior motive."

Having caught the pillow he lunged toward her and took her into his arms with a kiss, which sealed their agreement to leave the city and buy a house in Westchester where they could not only be closer to her father but also start a family.

NINE

HAVING HEARD OVER the loudspeaker that the train was arriving, Marika walked from the park to the front of the station. She heard the rumble of the train overhead, and then people started appearing from inside the station. She watched for Nina, who finally appeared, dressed in her usual high style. Marika advanced toward her daughter, and they hugged each other.

"How is she?" Nina asked.

"She's doing fine. She wants to come home."

"Well, that's good. When will they let her come home?"

"I don't know. They'll want to keep her until they're satisfied with her condition."

As they drove to the hospital they talked about Nina's job and about her boyfriend, with whom she had been living for almost three years. His name was Jack, and he was an associate at a law firm, working long hours in the hope of making partner. Marika liked him, and she hoped that sooner, rather than later, they would get married because Nina was twenty-nine, and Marika wanted her daughter to have time to settle down and have a family before reaching an age where she could have a problem getting pregnant.

They parked in the visitors' lot of the hospital, and before entering they put on the obligatory masks. She noticed that Nina, being a fashionista, had a stylish leopard-print mask instead of the standard surgical mask, and it made her smile.

When they reached the ICU floor they walked to the waiting area, where they found Frank. He got up and hugged Nina and complimented her on the mask. Since there was a two-person limit on visitors Marika and Nina went into the room to see Jessica, who brightened at the sight of her sister. As different as they were, they always had a good relationship, unlike Marika and her sister, and they started talking with the alacrity of two people who hadn't seen each other in a long time. After watching them and listening for a while Marika withdrew from the room so they could talk without being inhibited by a parent. She joined Frank in the waiting area and sat down next him.

"I'm glad Nina came to see her," he said.

"It perked her up," she said.

"You know, with all their differences they've always had a good relationship."

"They always have—unlike me and my sister."

"Yeah. Well, you and your sister live in different worlds."

"Jessica and Nina live in different worlds, but they engage with each other. And they don't compete with each other."

"Because they don't want the same thing."

"They don't. But they don't even compete for our attention."

"So maybe that's one thing we did right," he said. "We gave them equal attention."

"Actually," she said, "we give more attention to Jessica."

"We do when she gets into trouble."

"So could that be a motive for getting into trouble?"

"It could be. It gets her extra attention."

"It does. But she has a propensity for getting into trouble."

"Then you agree that to some extent she was born that way?"

"I guess I do, though I still feel I did something wrong."

"If you did something wrong," he said, "we both did. We're in this together."

About twenty minutes later Nina came out of the room and joined them. Before leaving, Marika and Frank went into the room and kissed Jessica goodnight.

They had dinner at an Italian restaurant on Odell Avenue, near the hospital, and while they were eating they asked Nina to tell them why she thought Jessica got into trouble.

"She gets into trouble," Nina told them without hesitation, "because she's always catfishing."

"What does that mean?" Marika asked.

"She goes on the internet to find people to have relationships with. She pretends she's someone else, not who she is."

"And who does she pretend she is?"

"She used to pretend she was a boy. But I don't know who she pretends to be now. She's looking for lesbians."

"So why doesn't she go to a bar where lesbians hang out?" Frank asked.

"I don't know," Nina said. "I guess she doesn't want people to know who she really is."

"And who is she really?" Marika asked.

Nina shook her head. "I don't think she knows who she is. And that's the problem. But at least she knows she's my sister."

"Thanks for coming," Frank said. "She was glad to see you."

"I wish I could help her, but I don't know how."

"We don't either," Marika said. "So don't feel bad about it. You came here to see her, and that helped a lot."

They left Nina at the train station in time for her to catch a train that would get her back into the city by ten, and then they drove home.

After sitting with Frank for a while to watch a Yankees game she went up to bed, and even after Frank joined her and fell asleep as usual by the count of ten she lay awake.

In the weeks that followed their decision to move to Yonkers so they would be closer to her father they looked for a house with the help of an agent whose office was on Palisade Avenue. The agent was an energetic woman in her fifties who knew the neighborhood and lined up houses for them to see on Saturdays and Sundays. Some of these houses were too large and some were too small while some were too far away from Marika's father, some were too close to him, and some were out of their price range. By the time their search was suspended by the holidays they hadn't found a house they liked and could afford, so they agreed with the agent to resume looking in January.

The holidays were grim. For Marika they were the first holidays without her mother, and that was bad enough but Julia kept making things worse. Instead of having Thanksgiving at her father's house, which was laden with memories, they accepted an invitation from Frank's parents to have Thanksgiving with them, and that helped a little, though it didn't help that Julia declined the invitation and spent Thanksgiving alone in the city. Marika and her father talked about having the Wigilia supper on Christmas Eve, but they decided not to and instead to have dinner at a Portuguese restaurant in Tarrytown, where they could have a meatless meal, and to go to church the next day at St. Brigid, which didn't have so many memories. And that helped a little, though it didn't help that Julia refused to join them, saying that as far as she was concerned there were no more Christmases.

During the last week of the year Marika finally reached Julia on the phone, and she tried to make Julia see how her behavior was making things worse for their father.

"What about me?" Julia said.

"I know it's hard for you," Marika said, feeling bad for her sister, "but it's hard for all of us."

"You and Dad have each other, but I have no one."

"That's not true. You have both of us."

"I don't. So leave me alone."

"But I don't want you to be alone. I love you."

Without responding Julia hung up.

The conversation left Marika feeling that somehow the impasse in her relationship with her sister was her fault, and she thought about it, trying to understand what she might have done to her sister, but she didn't get very far with it. And that night, as they were lying in bed, she told Frank about her conversation with Julia.

"It's not your fault," Frank assured her.

"You mean it's her fault?"

"It might not be anyone's fault. Your sister's being herself and you're being yourself, and neither of you can help it."

"That sounds like fate," Marika said, "and I don't want to think we're fated not to have a relationship."

"I understand. And I'm not saying you shouldn't keep trying to have a relationship with her. I'm only saying you shouldn't be so hard on yourself."

"Okay. But I just keep hoping that sooner or later we'll have a breakthrough."

"Maybe you will, but that depends on her as much as you. It goes both ways."

"I know it does. And I shouldn't let it get me down because I have to be there for my father."

"You always have me with you for that," Frank told her.

With the holidays over they resumed looking for a house, and in March they finally found one. It was on the other side of Roberts Avenue from her father, only about five minutes away by car. It was built of brick, which Frank liked because it would be relatively maintenance free. It had four bedrooms, so it would accommodate the children they hoped to have, and it had a backyard surrounded by a stockade fence, where their children could play safely. And it was near St. Brigid, which had an elementary school where their children could go..

Before committing to buy the house they asked their fathers to inspect it. Her father knew mechanical things, so he checked the boiler, the hot water heater, the refrigerator, and the window air conditioning units while his father knew buildings, so he checked the foundation, the walls, the windows, and the roof. Their fathers both approved of the house, though they both had a list of things that the seller should fix.

They signed the papers in early May by which time they had bought a car, a Ford station wagon that would easily accommodate her father and two or three children. It was a used car from a dealer that Frank's father trusted. Since they would be commuting they could use the car to get to the Yonkers train station, though they decided to try taking the bus there to see how that worked because if it did they could avoid the hassle of parking.

They hired a moving company on York Avenue to bring their furniture from the city. They had the essentials from Frank's apartment for the kitchen, the dining room, the living room, and one bedroom. They could also use the area rugs for the floors and the paintings for the walls, including the one of Stonington Harbor. They had plenty of time to get the other things they would need, so they weren't in any hurry.

They moved on a Friday, and they had her father at their house for dinner on Saturday evening. Frank cooked veal parmigiana, the dish her father always ordered at Italian restaurants, along with green beans and linguine with garlic and olive oil. With the food they drank a bottle of chianti, and to finish the meal they had a salad with olive oil and balsamic vinegar. Her father declared that it was better than eating in a restaurant.

On Sunday they met her father for the eleven o'clock Mass at St. Brigid, and afterward he drove them to the diner on Saw Mill River Road that they had been going to. The only difference was that now they were living in the area instead of only visiting, so Marika was more relaxed.

On Monday the bus was right on schedule and it got them to the train station with time to spare, so they decided not to use the car for that purpose. Since they were used to walking everywhere in the city, they walked to places as much as they could: to the shops on Palisade Avenue which included a supermarket, a pharmacy, a liquor store, a bank, and best of all an Italian deli that sold olive oil, fresh mozzarella, prosciutto, olives, and salted anchovies. Frank used the last item after rinsing off the salt for Caesar salad and pasta sauces.

They quickly settled into a routine of commuting to the city during the week and having her father at their house for dinner on Saturday night, or taking him out, and joining him for Mass at St. Brigid on Sunday, followed by brunch at the diner or occasionally at the Chart House in Dobbs Ferry. Marika somehow talked her sister into meeting them at the Chart House for brunch on a Sunday in the middle of June, and that went remarkably well—it helped that Julia had just been given a bonus for a deal that her team had done. And on the Fourth of July they took her father to a cookout at Frank's parents' house.

Like many other publishing companies, her company gave its employees Friday off during the summer, so she made an appointment for a Friday in late July to see the chairperson of the English department at St. Catherine College, which was north of St. John's Hospital. She couldn't drive because she still had to take the road test for her license, but it was a nice day, so she decided to walk if for no other reason than to see how long it took her to get there. She believed that with her master's degree from Hunter she would be qualified to teach as an adjunct at St. Catherine, and she hoped they might have an opening for that fall. In the back of her mind she envisioned someday getting a full-time job at St Catherine and having more time to spend with the children she hoped to have.

The office of the English department was in a stone building occupied by the School of Liberal Arts and Sciences. Inside the building Marika found the office of the chairperson, Mary O'Connor. She checked in with a secretary, who asked her to please be seated in a waiting area where two students were debating whether to take a course with a professor whose ratings were mixed. Within a few minutes a woman in her mid-forties with lively blue eyes appeared and headed toward her and introduced herself as Dr. O'Connor. Rising from the chair in which she had been sitting she introduced herself and followed the woman into an office. Among other things in the office she noticed a map of County Roscommon on the wall. She sat down in front of a desk while Dr. O'Connor went around and sat behind it. She had mailed her curriculum vitae to the college, and it was on the desk in front of Dr. O'Connor, who after taking a glance at it began the interview by saying: "Hunter has a great English program. We have several professors who got their master's degrees there."

She didn't comment, waiting for Dr. O'Connor to continue.

"And I see you did your thesis on Joseph Conrad. Do you think you could teach his short stories in a course?"

"I hadn't thought about it," Marika admitted. "But I guess I could."

"It would be a challenge, but we want our instructors to try different things. We don't want them to get complacent just teaching the usual short stories."

Again she didn't comment.

"So tell me why you want to teach an English course."

"I love reading," Marika said, straight from the heart, "and I want to help people learn to love reading as much as I do."

"That's a good reason. But why at St. Catherine?"

"You're a Catholic college, and I was raised with Catholic values."

"I can see that," Dr. O'Connor said, looking at her curriculum vitae. "You went to St. Casimir, Maria Regina, and Fordham. How did you happen to go to Hunter for your master's degree?"

"I was living in the city, so it was easy to get there. It was also less expensive than other colleges. And," she added, "I heard it had a great English program."

"So what do you know about St. Catherine?"

"I know you have students who are usually the first in their families to go to college."

"Were you the first in your family to go to college?"

"Oh, yes. My parents were both immigrants from Poland. In fact, they were refugees from the war. They didn't have it easy."

"So you think you could relate to our students?"

"I think I could. I grew up in Yonkers, where most of your students probably come from."

"Most of them do. But they also come from Mt. Vernon, the Bronx, and upper Manhattan. Do you speak any foreign languages?"

"I speak Polish."

"Did your family speak Polish at home?"

"Yes. I still speak it with my father."

"Is it fair to say that English is your second language?"

"I think it is. Some people say I have an accent."

"You do," Dr. O'Connor said, smiling. "But it's not a foreign accent, it's a Yonkers accent. Just for the record, I grew up in Inwood in what used to be an Irish neighborhood but now is a Dominican neighborhood. And while I lived there I learned some Spanish, though it wouldn't have been good enough for a literature course."

"I had a Puerto Rican roommate, and I learned some Spanish from her."

Over the next half hour Dr. O'Connor asked her questions, and finally after looking at a sheet of paper on her desk she said:

"Well, if you want it, I could give you an evening course in the fall. Our full-time faculty prefer to teach during the day, so I haven't filled all the evening courses. Would Thursday evening work for you?"

"Yes, it would. What time is the course?"

"It's from 6:15 to 9:05."

"What's the subject matter?"

"American short stories. This course is one of the two required English courses, so most of your students will be taking it because they have to, not because they want to."

"I understand," Marika said, remembering the students from Thayer's class. "And I don't have a problem with that."

"Then let's get you over to human resources so you can do the paperwork," Dr. O'Connor said, rising from her desk. "You have the course."

"Thank you so much."

An hour later she left the college with materials from the human resource department, a course syllabus for English 111, and a book for the course, which had been published by a rival of her company.

During the rest of the summer Marika worked on preparing her course. She followed the syllabus, and based on her experience at Fordham and her observation of Thayer's class, she decided on the weekly learning activities: reading a story, writing about it, and discussing it in class. She had always felt that mid-term exams and final exams were a waste of time, so instead she decided to have the students write a research paper on one of five possible topics, and to have them present their papers in the last two classes. She submitted her course outline to Dr. O'Connor by the middle of August, and it was accepted.

The first class was on the Wednesday after Labor Day, and it met in a classroom with windows that overlooked the Hudson River. There were nineteen students on her roster, only about half of whom were there at 6:15 when the class was supposed to begin. She gave them extra time to get there because she assumed that most of them were coming from work. As they gathered in the classroom she noticed that the guys mostly sat in the back while the girls mostly sat in the front as they had at Fordham, except that there the ratio of guys to girls was two-to-one whereas here it was the other way around, which made sense because St. Catherine had originally been a college for women.

By 6:25 there were twenty students in the classroom, so Marika began by introducing herself and taking attendance from the roster. The students were a mix of races and ethnic groups, with a plurality of Latinos but also a number with Irish and Italian names. Near the end of the roster she came to Małgorzata Wiśniewska, though the name didn't have the diacritics, and delighted to have a Polish girl in the class, she called out: "Małgorzata?"

"Maggie, Maggie," a girl told her. "Please call me Maggie."

The girl, who was sitting in the front row, had blond hair and blue eyes and a Slavic face with prominent cheekbones. She was wearing a loose-fitting blue top over faded jeans.

"Maggie? Okay," Marika said, marking the girl present.

When she had finished taking attendance she found that one of the students on the roster was absent, and two of the students present weren't on the roster, so she got their names and college ID numbers and wrote them down. Then, since this was the first class and the students didn't have assignments, she went over the course outline and explained to the students what she expected of them. She invited them to ask questions, but no one did, and she was done in less than an hour. Anticipating this situation she had copied the first page of a short story by John Cheever, which she handed out and asked the students to read in class. After giving them ample time to read it, she called on students from the roster, asking them questions about the reading, and in that way she got a few discussions going. Still, she let them out early, at the time when they would have taken a break, and reminding them to be sure to get the book from the bookstore, she watched them file out of the class. They all left except Maggie, who remained at her desk as if she had a question to ask the instructor.

"*Czy jesteś Polką?*" the girl asked her.

"My parents were Polish," she replied in Polish. Since she had written her name on the blackboard as Professor Bonetti she asked: "How did you guess?"

"You knew how to pronounce my name."

"So why do you want me to call you Maggie?"

"That's the name I use here. I don't want people to think I'm foreign."

Marika smiled. "Yeah, I know about that. My maiden name is Janczewski. Bonetti is my married name."

"You mean Janczewska," the girl corrected her. "You're female."

"You're right. Did you immigrate here with your family?"

"No. My family's in Poland."

"Then you're an international student?"

"Sort of. I mean—" The girl paused, and then with a sigh said: "It's a long story."

Since the class had ended early and Frank didn't expect her until after nine, she said: "If you have time I'd like to hear it."

"I have time," the girl said, getting up from the desk.

They went to the cafeteria, which was down the hall and down a flight of stairs. The girl got a coffee and Marika got a small bottle of water, and then they sat down at a corner table, away from a group of students who were carrying on.

Marika listened while the girl recounted what had happened to her. She was peacefully living in Warsaw, going to school, when the government declared martial law. She wasn't an activist, but like most students she dreamed of a future in which Poland was a free country. With the military cracking down on the least expression of dissent, her parents wanted to steer her clear of politics, so they encouraged her to join a group that performed traditional Polish dances, believing it would channel her energy and keep her out of trouble. She found that she loved dancing with the group, and it did keep her out of trouble until a friend who hung out with activists was arrested and thrown into prison. Her parents worried that somehow the government would find a connection between her and the friend, so when the group was invited to go on an international tour they saw an opportunity for her to escape from Poland to a country where she could have a better life. They contacted an exile in Paris, where the group was scheduled to perform, and they asked him to give her a temporary safe haven while he got her a visa, and then to book her on a flight to New York, where they had relatives. Everything happened according to plan, and Maggie arrived in the middle of June. The relatives lived in Hastings, and since she had a high school diploma with good grades she applied to St. Catherine and was accepted based on the recommendation of a nun from the Polish order that had two schools in Westchester County.

"Really?" Marika said. "Were the schools St. Casimir and Maria Regina?"

"Yeah, how did you know?"

"I went to both schools, and I probably had the nun as a teacher. What's her name?"

"Sister Franciszka."

"I did have her. She encouraged my interest in reading."

"That's amazing," Maggie said. "Or maybe it isn't. Maybe it was planned."

"Whatever it was, I'm glad to have you in my class. But what about your parents? Did they get into trouble for helping you escape from Poland?"

"The government took away their passports, so they're stuck in Poland. But they didn't want to leave anyway. They only wanted to get me out of there so I could have a better life."

"You must miss them."

"I do miss them, but I'm hoping to go back there within a few years when Poland is a free country."

"You believe it will happen that soon?"

"Yeah. I know it will. We have the Pope on our side."

By the end of the month the students sorted themselves out into a bimodal distribution of those who were doing an excellent job and those who weren't doing the work. The latter were almost ten percent of the class, so Marika gave them special attention and tried to help them overcome obstacles, and she rescued about half of them. Despite the fact that English was her second language Maggie stood out among the students who were doing an excellent job. Her papers were so well written that without identifying the author Marika shared a few of them with the class as examples of what she expected of students, and she thought it helped to raise the overall level of performance.

She had told Frank about Maggie, and they had discussed the possibility of inviting the girl for dinner on a Saturday, with the idea that her father would enjoy meeting someone fresh from Poland. Marika had put off inviting her because she didn't want it to look like she was favoring a student, but after seeing how well Maggie performed she stopped worrying about that issue, and she invited Maggie for dinner toward the end of October.

Maggie's relatives were a couple who like Marika's parents had immigrated from Poland after the war. The man had worked at the Anaconda plant in Hastings and like Marika's father had lost his job when the plant closed. The woman was a nurse at St. John's Hospital. For a while they had lived in Yonkers and then they moved to Hastings after the birth of their second child. They attended St. Stanislaw, a Polish church in Hastings affiliated with St. Casimir. It occurred to Marika that her father would also enjoy meeting them because they had a lot in common, so she invited them as well.

The dinner went well. In fact, it was Marika's first success in getting her father to socialize outside his family. For months she had been urging him to join the senior citizens group that met weekly at the Polish Center, and it turned out that Maggie's relatives attended those meetings, and they convinced her father to join them. Her father and the man shared their experience of losing good jobs at companies where they had worked for many years, they talked about the priest who had been transferred from St. Casimir to St. Stanislaw, and then they got into the subject of Poland, which was still suffering under the repression of martial law. Though the men were pessimistic about the situation, Maggie was optimistic based on recent information from a friend that the resistance movement was getting stronger, and that a charismatic leader had emerged. His name was Lech Wałęsa, who the friend predicted would lead Poland to freedom from Russia. In the heat of this conversation they had lapsed into Polish, so Marika had to translate for Frank and finally guide them back into English. Their guests stayed until almost eleven, and after Frank returned from driving her father home they sat on the sofa in the living room, sipping sambuca, reflecting on the evening, and resolving to repeat the experience.

Now that they were settled in the house they decided it was time to start a family, so she went off the pill and tried to get pregnant. After several months of trying without success Marika saw a gynecologist whose office was across the street from St. John's Hospital. He examined her thoroughly and found no reason why she couldn't get pregnant, but after several more months of trying she began to wonder if there was something wrong with her. The doctor gave her a series of tests and recommended that Frank get tested, which he promptly did. When the tests failed to identify a problem the doctor advised her to keep trying.

They did keep trying all through the fall and the following spring, but nothing happened. In the meantime she was offered a full-time position at St. Catherine with the understanding that she would get a Ph. D., and she accepted. During that summer she was preparing her courses for the fall when her gynecologist referred her to a doctor in the city who specialized in fertility problems. She made an appointment on a Friday before the fall semester began. The doctor's name was Edita Vesely, and her office was in the East Sixties on the ground floor of an apartment building. Instead of a girl at the reception desk there was a man in his fifties with very thick glasses and an accent that sounded English. Fussing around the reception area were two small Yorkshire terriers, one with a blue bow on his head and the other with a pink bow, presumably a boy and a girl.

The man gave her papers to fill out, which sitting in a chair she duly completed while the dogs investigated her. After handing in the papers she didn't have to wait long before a young woman in nurse's scrubs came out and led her back into an office, where she was greeted by Dr. Vesely, a petite woman with perfectly coiffed blond hair and sky blue eyes. She was very well dressed, with tasteful jewelry and refined makeup. In the open neck of her flowered blouse a gold cross, hanging from a delicate gold chain, was visible but not obtrusive.

"Before we get started," the doctor said with a noticeable foreign accent, "let me give you my background. I grew up in Prague, where I studied medicine, and then I went to London for my residency. I practiced in London for a while, and then I came here and did further studies in my specialization. I've had this practice for more than twenty years, so I can give you the benefit of my experience but I can't guarantee that you will get pregnant."

"I understand," Marika said.

After glancing at the papers on her desk the doctor said: "So you're thirty-one now, and you've been trying for how long?"

"Since I went off the pill last fall."

"And your health is good?"

"I don't have any health problems, at least that I know of."

"If you don't know of them," the doctor told her with a faint smile, "you probably don't have them. But I will examine you thoroughly and do some tests so that we can rule out the usual problems. Is that okay?"

"Yeah, it's okay," Marika said.

"My nurse will take you to an examining room, where you can make yourself comfortable." At that point the doctor must have pressed a buzzer because within a few minutes the nurse appeared.

She spent the next hour being examined by the doctor and giving blood samples. When they were finally done she went back into the doctor's office, where she waited for the verdict, fearing the worst.

"From what I could see," the doctor told her, "Everything looks fine, though we have to wait for the results of the blood tests."

"*Dzięki Bogu*," she barely whispered.

"That sounded like Polish," the doctor said, interested. "Are you Polish?"

"My parents are. I mean my father is, and my mother was."

"Did you lose your mother?"

"She died two years ago."

"I'm very sorry," the doctor said, pausing for a while and then saying: "That could be a factor. Are you under a lot of stress now?"

"I guess I am. I worry about my father, and I just started a new job, so——" She trailed off.

"Well, let's see what the tests say, but if we don't find anything physiological, then the problem could be psychological."

"Could being under stress prevent a woman from getting pregnant?"

"It could," the doctor said. "At least being under stress could make it harder."

"So I need to reduce the stress in my life?"

"Yes. Or change the way you handle it. Are you doing regular exercise?"

"I was, but I haven't done any since we moved to Yonkers."

"Then you should get into a program. I do Pilates."

"Okay. I'll look into it," she said, having heard about that exercise system.

They talked for a while longer about stress and handling it, and she left with some material that explained how to monitor ovulation by using a thermometer.

She began taking her temperature every morning, and Frank recorded it in a spreadsheet that he had created. They watched for the temperature that indicated ovulation, and they made love at that time. They jokingly referring to it as "sex on demand," but they never failed to take advantage of an optimal temperature.

In the meantime she found a Pilates studio in Dobbs Ferry, and she began taking classes there. The exercises were similar to the ones she had done in the city, and she had no trouble adapting to them. Her classes at the college were in the late morning and the early afternoon, so she could get to the studio in time for the five o'clock exercise class, which she did twice a week. The instructor, a no-nonsense woman from Brazil, was a taskmaster, but Marika appreciated the discipline, and when she got home on those evenings and found Frank in the kitchen cooking dinner she felt free of stress, which he could verify by checking the muscles in her shoulders as he gave her a warm homecoming hug.

During that fall she applied to the doctoral program in English literature at CUNY with recommendations from Dr. O'Connor and her adviser for the master's program at Hunter College. In early December she interviewed with the director of the doctoral program, and two weeks later she received a letter of acceptance.

For the holidays they did what they had been doing for the past two years, and this time Julia joined them for dinner at the Portuguese restaurant on Christmas Eve, she spent the night at their father's house, and she went to Mass at St. Brigid with them the next day. She still talked about the money she was making, but not as much, and she even showed an interest in Marika's professional life as well as in their father's social life. It left Marika with the feeling that her sister was beginning to recognize the value of her family.

During that spring they continued trying to have a baby, always monitoring her ovulation with the thermometer and the spreadsheet. At one time in February the data indicated that she might be pregnant, but their hopes were dashed by a period. Beginning to wonder if Dr. Vesely could have missed something, Marika made an appointment to see her in early April. After another thorough examination and more tests the doctor told her she still hadn't found any physiological problem and recommended that she and her husband go on vacation for at least two weeks, ideally where there was nothing to do but rest and relax. So for two weeks in May after she submitted her grades for the spring semester they booked a trip at the hotel in the Dominican Republic where they had stayed a few years ago.

It made a difference to have two weeks instead of only one, and by the second week she was so relaxed that she didn't know what day it was. There were sunny mornings. leisurely lunches, long siestas, romantic dinners, and quiet nights of blissful sleep.

By the middle of June the data indicated that Marika was pregnant, and this time their hopes weren't dashed by a period. She made an appointment with Dr. Vasely, who confirmed that she was indeed pregnant. Before leaving, she hugged the doctor and joyfully petted the Yorkshire terriers, and on the way home from the train station she stopped at St. Brigid, where she lit a candle for the Blessed Mother and gave thanks.

Her due date was in March, so she asked for a maternal leave during that spring. After some discussion with Dr. O'Connor they agreed that she should take the whole semester off and resume her position in the fall. They also agreed that she should keep working on her doctoral degree, which she had begun in January with the plan of doing her dissertation on what Joseph Conrad brought to the English novel from his Polish background. She spent that summer preparing her courses for the fall and working on her dissertation proposal, a draft of which she submitted to her advisor by the end of August. Her advisor liked the proposal, making only a few suggestions to improve it.

The fall flew by, and as her due date approached she was conscious of a rising level of stress, which she handled by going to Pilates classes as long as she could. The Brazilian woman who taught the classes assured her that the exercises were beneficial for pregnant women despite being designed by a man, and she didn't stop the classes until the end of February.

The doctor who had referred her to Dr. Vesely delivered the baby at St. John's Hospital on March 17, a date which would have been significant if she had been Irish. The baby was a girl, who according to her father looked like Marika when she was a baby. She and Frank had agreed not to give the baby a name from either of their families, and after they considered calling her Patricia in honor of St. Patrick's Day they decided to call her Jessica. Her father questioned whether Jessica was a saint's name, so she asked one of her professors from Fordham if there was such a saint. The professor told her that by a stretch of the imagination one could claim that Jessica was related to Joanna, which was a saint's name, and that satisfied her father. When the baby was almost three months old she was baptized at St. Brigid with Julia as godmother. The priest, Father Paul, slipped and used the name Joanna, at the sound of which the baby swung a tiny, chubby fist at him. Marika politely corrected him, though it made her wonder if they should have named the baby Joanna.

Afterward at the family party, which they had at an Irish pub on Lake Avenue, they had a good laugh at the swing that Jessica had taken at the priest. Her father, who was drinking shots of vodka, predicted that his granddaughter would be a prize fighter, and Frank's father said her nickname should be Lefty. Marika laughed with them, but for her the incident confirmed what she already knew—that Jessica was a difficult baby. At feeding time she refused the nourishment that Marika offered her. At nap time she refused to sleep. When they put her in a crib with bunnies and bears she tossed the animals out onto the floor. And at times for no reason that they could imagine she would scream at a level to awaken the dead. Since her father had said that Jessica looked like her as a baby Marika asked him if she had been a difficult baby, and he said no, she had been an easy baby, whereas Julia had been a difficult baby, making her wonder if Jessica had inherited something from her family that made her difficult.

TEN

THE NEXT MORNING they found Jessica unhooked from the lines and out of bed, walking around to test her legs. The nurse was standing by in case she needed help. They only spent about five minutes in the room before the doctor appeared and asked them to leave while he examined Jessica. They went to the waiting area, which had no other occupants now so they could talk.

"She looks good," Frank said. "So maybe they'll release her tomorrow."

"Well, let's see what the doctor says," Marika cautioned him. Frank always took an optimistic view while she always took a pessimistic view, which worked because it kept them in balance, not veering one way or the other.

About a half hour later the doctor found them and gave them his view, saying: "She's mostly recovered, so she can go home tomorrow."

"That's great," Frank said.

"Is she on any medicine?" Marika asked.

"Yes. I'll give you prescriptions. The most important thing is for her to get plenty of rest and not exert herself in any way."

"She'll be at home with us," Frank said.

"I'm off work for the summer," Marika said "so I'll be there with her."

"Well, it goes without saying, she shouldn't drink alcohol or take any recreational drugs. We don't want her to have a relapse."

"We'll keep a close eye on her." Frank said.

With a frown the doctor asked: "Have you heard anything from the police?"

"No, not since their phone call." Marika told him.

"Then they probably don't have a trail on the person who gave your daughter fentanyl."

"She said it was someone she met on the internet."

"It's always someone they meet on the internet," the doctor muttered. "What a messed-up world we've given our kids."

Though Marika didn't feel she had messed up the world she did feel that somehow she had messed up her kid, so the doctor's comment hit a sore point. Still, she was grateful to him for saving Jessica's life, and she whole-heartedly thanked him.

After spending about an hour with Jessica they left the hospital. Frank took the car to go to White Plains for a meeting with the developer of his latest project, and Marika walked home. On the way she continued thinking about the past, remembering how difficult Jessica had been as a baby. The saving grace was that Maggie, who had become like a member of the family, helped her take care of Jessica, coming to the house and playing with Jessica, always speaking to her in Polish, which for some reason calmed her down, and they joked about making a tape of Maggie talking in Polish that they could play at night to help Jessica go to sleep.

On one of her visits Maggie brought some color photos of her dance group. One photo showed Maggie in a traditional costume: a white blouse, an embroidered vest, a full floral skirt, a white apron, and lace-up red leather boots. Her blond hair was braided up in a crown, graced by a flower wreath with ribbons. Another photo showed her with four other girls, all wearing the same costume, and another showed them dancing with guys who were also wearing traditional costumes.

"In that photo we were doing the krakowiak," Maggie said.

"I sort of learned to do that," Marika said. "What other dances did you do?"

"The kujawiak, the mazurka, the oberek, and of course the polonaise."

"Wow. Did you like dancing?"

"Oh, yeah. And at times I miss it. But I can't complain. It got me out of Poland."

Maggie left the photos so Marika could show them to her father, and looking at them she remembered how her father dressed her in a traditional costume when she was around three years old. He took her to the Polish Center and stood her on the bar proudly for everyone to see. At the time she liked the attention but she didn't understand that for them she was a symbol of Poland, an outpost of Western civilization that over the centuries had been overrun repeatedly by barbarian hordes and now was occupied by savage Russians.

Three months after Jessica was born there were elections in Poland, and Lech Wałęsa won in a landslide. Poland finally became a free, independent country, and they had a party to celebrate at the Polish Center, with food and beer and vodka and dancing. Marika especially enjoyed watching her father do the polka with Maggie, who had never looked happier.

Almost three years later Marika had her second baby, whom they named Nina after no one in their families. Frank's mother said she looked like Frank when he was a baby, and there was no doubt about where she got her dark eyes and her dark hair. And Nina was an easy baby, completely different from Jessica despite having the same parents.

"Was Frank an easy baby?" Marika asked his mother while his parents and her father were having dinner at her house.

"Oh, he was okay," his mother said, "but his brother was the easy one."

"Easier than Frank?"

"Yeah. But Frank wasn't difficult."

"So all families don't have a difficult baby?"

"Our family did," her father said, referring to Julia.

Intrigued, she asked him: "Would you say there are similarities between Jessica and Julia?"

"Yeah. But there are also differences."

"What are the similarities?"

"They both act more like boys than girls."

"And what are the differences?"

"Well, for one thing," her father said, "Jessica engages with people. She doesn't always engage well, but at least she engages, while Julia avoids engaging."

Marika was impressed by his analysis. "So how can we get Julia to engage?"

"I don't know. I guess we could try to get her to engage as a godmother."

"Yeah, we could. Should we ask her to be Nina's godmother."

"I think it makes sense," Frank said.

"If they both have the same godmother," his mother said, "it'll simplify things for you."

So she called Julia the next day and asked her to be Nina's godmother, and after determining her availability for the baptism Julia agreed.

Now with a three-year-old and a baby they continued going to the eleven o'clock Mass, picking up her father in their station wagon and sitting in their usual pew. They had breakfast after Mass at the usual diner, where her father always had scrambled eggs, bacon, and toasted whole wheat bread while Jessica had pancakes and Nina had a bottle. As the girls got older Jessica had waffles and Nina had French toast. By now the waiters at the diner, who were members of an extended Greek family, knew in advance what they were going to have but always gave them a chance to order something else. After breakfast they drove her father back to their house, where he spent the afternoon watching sports on television with Frank. He tolerated football and basketball, but he really liked baseball, and he had become a loyal Yankees fan.

Maggie graduated in the spring of the year when Nina was born, and though she could now go back to Poland she stayed for a while to help with Nina and also to help with Jessica, who needed extra attention to help her adjust to no longer being the only child. When she thought back on this period Marika believed that it was the extra attention from Maggie that prevented Jessica from being jealous of the new baby and laid a foundation for the relationship that Jessica and Nina developed. As they grew up they almost always got along with each other, and Marika wished she had such a good relationship with Julia.

The girls were six and three years old when Marika completed her doctoral degree, and they were still as different as ever. Jessica liked physical activities, which mostly involved sports, whereas Nina liked social activities, which mostly involved dolls and friends.

There were a lot of kids in the neighborhood, so they didn't have any trouble finding local playmates for their preferred activities, and Marika didn't have to cart them around for play sessions with kids who lived beyond walking distance the way a lot of suburban mothers did. She only had to keep an eye on the kids or make sure another mother was keeping an eye on them, as her own mother had done while she and Julia were growing up on Nodine Hill.

Jessica had gone to kindergarten at St. Brigid School, and she continued going there. The school was within walking distance from their house, but Marika drove her there because of the traffic on Roberts Avenue which Jessica would have to cross. By third grade there were girls her age in the neighborhood who walked to school, so Marika let her go with them. By then Nina was in kindergarten, so in the morning she went with Jessica, but since her school day ended at noon Marika picked her up and brought her home. Luckily, she was always able to schedule her courses around her responsibilities as a mother.

When Jessica was in third grade she got into trouble. In previous years she had been characterized as "aggressive" by her teachers, but that was based on things she said to other students, not on physical actions, so there hadn't been any major consequences. And she had been characterized as "very respectful" by her religious education teachers. So Marika was a little surprised when she got a phone call from the principal of St. Brigid School asking her to come and meet with her and the third grade teacher that afternoon to discuss Jessica's behavior.

The principal was a nun, a woman in her mid-sixties with austere gray eyes, and the teacher was a woman in her early forties with auburn hair and mirthful green eyes. The teacher's name was Sara Solís, though that must have been her married name because she looked Irish. After the preliminaries the nun asked Sara to recount what had happened.

The class had eighteen students about equally divided between girls and boys, whom Sara assigned regular seats that mixed the genders so they wouldn't always sit together in groups of all girls and all boys. From the beginning Sara had noticed that Jessica tended to avoid the boys and hang out with the girls at recess, which was normal at that age. Except for an occasional remark in reaction to something a boy had said to her, Jessica hadn't done anything physical until yesterday when she had hit a boy on the playground hard enough to give him a black eye.

"This happened yesterday?" Marika said.

"Yeah. It happened during the morning recess."

"So why didn't you call me yesterday?"

"I heard what the boy said to her," Sara told her, "and in my opinion it deserved a reaction, though she shouldn't have hit him."

"We teach the children not to commit acts of violence," the nun said.

"I talked with Jessica," Sara said. "She admitted doing it, and she was sorry, and I got her to apologize to the boy."

"Did she hurt him badly?"

"No, not really. I mean she gave him a black eye, but from what I could see there wasn't any serious damage."

"Unfortunately," the nun informed her, "his mother called and complained about it."

"So you have to punish Jessica?"

"Yes. We have to put her on probation."

"She has to understand that there are consequences for bad behavior," Sara said, "but I don't think punishment is the solution."

"What's the solution?"

"Jessica is a physical girl, and from what I've observed she has a lot of pent-up energy. If our school had sports teams she could expend that energy playing sports."

"We have CYO teams," the nun said.

"But only in basketball," Sara said, "which I don't think is the right channel for her."

"What do you think would be the right channel?"

"I think karate."

"Karate?"

"Yeah. It would give her a way to expend energy, and it would teach her how to control her aggression. I know about it," Sara explained, "because I've had other students who had trouble controlling their aggression, and karate helped them."

"Were they boys or girls?" Marika asked.

"They were boys, but if karate helps boys it could also help girls. In fact, there's a karate school in Hastings, and almost half the kids are girls."

"How old are they?"

"From six to eighteen."

"Do you know the teacher?"

"I know him well. He's the assistant baseball coach at St. Catherine College."

"Really? I'm a professor there."

"Then you might know him. His name is Deylin Cabrera."

Marika knew the name but had never met him. "Okay, thanks. I'll contact him."

At that point the nun excused herself, and freed from her presence Marika and Sara began talking and discovering things they had in common. Like her, Sara grew up in Yonkers and went to Fordham and got a job in the city and moved there. Like her, Sara lost her mother at an early age and moved back to Yonkers to take care of her father and have a family. Like her, Sara married someone outside of her community. Like her, Sara had a younger sister who made a lot of money and didn't help her with their father. And like her, Sara had problems getting pregnant and was treated by the same fertility specialist, Dr. Vesely. The main difference was that Sara was finally unable to have a baby because of endometriosis, so she adopted one from the Dominican Republic, where her husband was from.

Sara told her that during the years when she was trying to get pregnant she had found it helpful to talk with Father Paul. Above all it had helped her keep her faith through a difficult time. And she suggested that it might be helpful for Marika to talk with him about Jessica and share her concerns with him.

When she got home she found Jessica in her room sitting on the floor, assiduously doing a school project. She sat down with Jessica and watched her for a while and then said: "I got a call from the school today asking me to meet with the principal and your teacher, Mrs. Solís."

Jessica kept working as if she hadn't heard.

"Do you like Mrs. Solís?"

"Yeah." Jessica kept working, drawing a series of boxes on a sheet of paper.

"Why do you like her?"

"I don't know. She likes kids."

"She likes you."

"How do you know?"

"I could tell from the way she talked about you."

Jessica said nothing, but she finally stopped working.

"They told me you hit a boy on the playground yesterday."

"Yeah. I did. But he deserved it."

"Why did he deserve it?"

"He called me a loser."

"Why did that upset you so much?"

"Because sometimes I feel like a loser."

"But you're good at everything you do. And we all love you," Marika added, putting an arm around her shoulder.

"Even though I can be a pain in the ass?"

Marika smiled. "Who did you hear that from?"

"Grampa. But he didn't mean it. He was just kidding me."

"Then you didn't take it seriously?"

"Oh, no. I know Grampa loves me. I mean, he calls me *moja Polska dziewczynka.*"

"That's what he called me when I was your age."

"So am I like you?" Jessica asked, finally facing her.

"You look like me, and in some respects you're like me, but in other respects you're different from me."

"How am I different?"

"You're more aggressive."

Jessica nodded as if she agreed.

"What I talked about with Mrs. Solís was finding a way to channel your energy and control your aggression. Do you understand?"

"I think I do."

"And she suggested doing karate. Do you know what that is?"

"Is it what Bruce Lee does in movies?"

"Where did you see a Bruce Lee movie?"

"In the living room with Dad," Jessica said, "while you were upstairs correcting papers."

She should have guessed. "So what do you think about the idea of taking karate classes?"

"I think it would be cool."

"Then we'll go and check it out. They have a karate school in Hastings. But in the meantime don't hit people no matter what they say to you. Okay?"

"Okay."

"And remember," she added, "the boy who called you a loser yesterday, he's the loser, not you. Winners don't say nasty things to other people."

They ended the conversation with a long warm hug.

She called Deylin Cabrera the next day and arranged for her, Frank, and Jessica to visit a class on Saturday morning. They drove to Hastings and parked in a lot with diagonal spaces and old mechanical meters. The karate school was on the main street in a building that had once been a movie theater and had been divided into units for stores. The school had ample space on a plain wooden floor, and when they arrived a class was just beginning. A woman at the desk invited them to sit down in folding chairs at one end of the room, where they could watch the class and be out of the way.

The teacher, presumably Deylin, wore a black uniform with a black headband and a black belt around his waist. The students, who wore white uniforms and belts of different colors, were kneeling on the floor and sitting upright. As they went through the warmup exercises, obeying the teacher's commands and responding in Japanese phrases, Marika was impressed with how disciplined the students were, including a few who looked around six. After the warmup exercises the students practiced prescribed routines and then in pairs they sparred with each other. The final event was a sparring match between the teacher and a boy with a brown belt who looked about eighteen. From the way that Jessica watched them spar, not missing a single punch or kick, Marika could tell she was engaged.

After the class they talked with Deylin, who explained the program and gave them the schedule. By then they were ready to sign up Jessica, but she requested that her father do the classes with her. Unprepared and not wanting to have a family discussion in front of Deylin, they excused themselves and went outside to talk among themselves.

"This is for you," Marika told Jessica.

"You don't need me," Frank said. "And anyway I'm thirty years older than the oldest kid in that class. Who would I spar with?"

"You could spar with the teacher," Jessica said.

"No, I couldn't. I'm not in his league."

"But you told me you did martial arts when you were in the marines."

"Yeah, but it wasn't karate. Though I guess it had elements of karate," he added. "Still, that was a long time ago."

"Just do it for one year," Jessica pleaded.

Marika and Frank exchanged a look in which it was decided that he should do it for Jessica, and they went back into the school and signed up, with Frank lying about his age and saying he was only thirty-five.

Having made an appointment to see Father Paul the following Thursday in the afternoon, she drove from the college to St. Brigid and parked in the lot for parishioners. She was greeted at the rectory by the woman who had made the appointment for her. She recognized the woman from seeing her at the eleven o'clock Mass, and she followed her into an office where she found Father Paul sitting at his desk. An attractive man in his early sixties with wavy silver-streaked dark hair and cheery blue eyes, he rose from his chair immediately and invited her to sit in an area that had a small sofa and two chairs. She sat down in one of the chairs, and he sat down in the other.

She had been attending Mass at this church since her family moved to the neighborhood from Nodine Hill, and she knew that Father Paul had come from Ireland years ago and served at a parish in the north of the county before being assigned to St. Brigid. He spoke with a brogue, and he often used stories from his home country to illustrate points in his homilies. Marika had talked with him on many occasions and even occasionally in confessions but never in a consultation, so she felt a little awkward, not knowing how to begin the conversation.

"How's your father?" the priest asked her, taking the initiative.

"He's fine," she said. "He likes your homilies."

"He does? He never told me."

"My father's not long on compliments, but in his own way he shows appreciation for the things he likes."

"Yeah, I know what kind of cigar he likes."

"You do?" She was surprised. "How?"

"At times he walks by when I'm out in front taking a break, and he stops to talk. I've learned a lot of history from him."

Father Paul was notorious for taking cigarette breaks in front of the church, where he talked with people passing by, and she could easily imagine her father stopping to talk while they indulged together in nicotine. "The history of Poland?"

The priest nodded. "It's like the history of Ireland. They were both colonies of powerful, imperial neighbors."

"They were," she agreed. "And they shed a lot of blood to become independent."

"God rest their souls." Father Paul leaned toward her in a listening mode. "But you didn't come here to talk about wars of independence. What's on your mind?"

She collected herself. "Well, as you know I was raised as a Catholic, and I'm trying to raise my children as Catholics, but I feel like I'm failing."

"Failing? How? I see your children with you in church."

"They come to church, but one of them has problems, and my faith is being challenged."

"Is it the older one?" he asked.

"Yes." She wondered if Father Paul had heard about what Jessica did at the school, or if he remembered Jessica throwing a punch at him while he baptized her.

"So how is your faith being challenged?"

"Well, I want to believe that God has a plan for my daughter, but I don't see how her behavior could be in his plan."

"What kind of behavior?"

"Being so aggressive."

"Can you give me an example?"

"Yeah, what she did last week to a boy at school."

"What did she do?"

"You haven't heard about it?"

"No, I haven't."

"She hit him and gave him a black eye."

He frowned. "She did? Why did she hit him?"

"He called her a loser."

"A loser? Mm. Is that a particular sore point for her?"

"Being called a loser? Yeah, it is. At times she feels like a loser."

"How do you know?"

"She told me. And if she feels like a loser, it's my fault."

He paused, then asked: "How is it your fault?"

"Well, as her mother," she said, "I should instill a feeling of self-worth in her."

"You should try, but as her mother you can only do so much. You can't do everything."

"I still feel it's my fault. I feel there's something I've done or failed to do that makes her feel like a loser."

He looked doubtful. "You said she hit the boy who called her a loser. Was she always so aggressive?"

"Oh, yeah, from the very beginning. Don't you remember her throwing a punch at you while you baptized her?"

"I remember a punch being thrown," he said, smiling, "but I don't remember which baby it was. So it was Jessica?"

"Yeah, it was Jessica."

"Then maybe she was born that way."

"My husband thinks she was."

The priest looked at her knowingly. "But you don't think so. You think you did something to make her that way."

"I feel I did, but I don't know what. I know I'm not a perfect mother, but I love her, and I want what's best for her."

"Do you know what's best for her?"

"No, I don't. But I want what's best for her, whatever it is." She added: "I believe that God knows what's best for her, but he doesn't reveal what it is. And I don't see how her being so aggressive could be in his plan."

The priest nodded. "I know it may be hard for us to see how something could be in God's plan, but we have to trust that he knows what he's doing."

"That's my problem," she said, getting to the bottom of it. "I don't trust that God knows what he's doing with Jessica."

The priest sighed. "I must admit, there are times when I don't trust that God know what he's doing with people."

"You don't? And how do you deal with it?"

"I pray without ceasing."

"I pray a lot, but maybe not enough. I guess I spend more time worrying about Jessica than praying for her."

"When you pray for her, pray for yourself."

"For myself? For what?"

"For faith," he told her. "For trust that God knows what he's doing with her."

"Okay," she said after taking that in. "But I can't just sit back and trust that God knows what he's doing with her. I mean, I'm her mother. I have to do something."

"I understand. So tell me, is your daughter unhappy?"

"At times she is, but at times she's happy."

"What makes her happy?"

"Helping people makes her happy."

"Then maybe you should try to find opportunities for her to help people."

She considered. "Yeah. I can imagine how she would be good in a career where she could help people, but I don't want to push her into anything. She's only eight."

"Does she get along with her younger sister?"

"Oh, yeah. Of course she had to adjust to not being the only child, but she got over it."

"So they have a good relationship?"

"They have a very good relationship."

"Well, that's a blessing." The priest paused. "Now, what have you done about her aggressive behavior?"

"We enrolled her in karate school."

He smiled brightly. "Did Sara suggest it?"

"Yeah, she said it helped some kids, so we decided to try it."

"I've watched those classes, and I think the discipline of karate can help kids. It certainly doesn't hurt them. So maybe karate is in God's plan for your daughter."

"Maybe. I just wish I knew what his plan is."

"You and every other parent," he said with understanding. "Whatever God's plan is, you're doing your part by loving your daughter. But remember, it's not your plan, so you don't determine its outcome. Also remember, your faith will be challenged, but if you keep loving your daughter and hoping for her, then everything will fall into place."

She thanked Father Paul, and she left the rectory feeling better. She resolved to pray more and to look for opportunities where Jessica could help people.

It happened shortly after Jessica had started high school at Maria Regina, which she liked because it was only girls. She commuted there by bus, as Marika had, but she didn't mind, and she made new friends while riding the bus. The opportunity for babysitting arose with the family a few doors away who had two children, five and seven. The father was a plumber with his own business, and the mother ran the office at home, making appointments, sending bills, collecting payments, and managing the bank account. Her name was Gail, and after working and cooking all week she liked to go out for dinner on Saturday night. Her problem was finding a babysitter who could deal with her kids, who were notorious for being not only difficult but also, in the words of one neighbor, impossible. So they had trouble finding babysitters, and if they found one they had trouble keeping her.

One day, as Marika was walking past their house on her way to buy food on Palisade Avenue, she was stopped by Gail, who after some preliminary conversation asked if Jessica would be interested in babysitting her kids that Saturday. Since Jessica had never done any babysitting before, except informally with her younger sister, Marika told Gail she would ask Jessica and get back to her.

When she got home from shopping she told Jessica about the opportunity, and Jessica said she was interested. So they arranged for her to babysit Gail's kids.

That Saturday, as she and Frank were watching television, she kept expecting a phone call from Jessica, but there was no phone call, and when Jessica got home shortly after ten she was beaming with satisfaction.

"How were the kids?" Marika asked.

"Oh, they were fine," Jessica said happily. "I didn't have any problem with them."

Gail confirmed this assessment the next day when she called and thanked Marika for the best babysitter they ever had, and from then on Jessica sat those kids on a regular basis. In fact, her reputation spread through the neighborhood to a point where she had to turn down business. Clearly, she had a way with kids, a natural ability to relate with them. After wondering where it had come from, Marika decided it was simply a gift from God.

Jessica continued going to karate classes through high school, and Frank continued going with her until he got a brown belt, at which point he announced that he had gone far enough with karate. By then Jessica no longer needed his support because she had the support of Deylin, who dreamed of her being the first girl in his dojo to get a black belt.

Meanwhile Nina was developing differently. Since the age of five she had shown an interest in shoes, clothes, and accessories, and she had become what Jessica called a "girly-girl." But they got along fine, maybe because they weren't competing in the same areas, and it helped that they didn't have to share a bedroom. One notable difference was that Jessica had more of a relationship with her grandfather, nurtured by playing poker with him and scratching the numbers of his lotto tickets. He still called her *moja Polska dziewczynka,* and he still said other things to her in Polish, whereas he only spoke English to Nina. He said that Nina had a fine sense of style, and he predicted that she would go far in the fashion industry.

Jessica was in her junior year of high school, preparing to go for her black belt, when Marika got a phone call from the Yonkers police who told her that Jessica had been apprehended for theft from a downtown store. Since Frank was still at work she left Nina in front of the television and drove to the downtown police station, where she managed to get Jessica released after hearing a lecture from an officer about not letting children run wild. The only specific information he gave her was that Jessica had been caught stealing a baseball from a sporting goods store on Main Street.

As she drove home with Jessica beside her in the passenger seat she began the conversation by asking: "Why did you steal a baseball?"

After a pause Jessica said: "Because they told me to."

"Who told you?"

"The girls in this club."

"Club? What club?"

"It's a club you can only get into if you pass some tests."

"And stealing a baseball was one of these tests?"

"Yeah. It was the first test."

"What are the next tests?"

"I don't know," Jessica said unhappily. "And they won't tell me now because I failed the first test."

"How did you fail?"

"I got caught."

Marika slowed for a red light. "You mean you were supposed to get away with it?"

"Yeah."

"Well, I want to know more about these girls. Where did you meet them?"

"On the internet. They have a website."

They had bought computers for the girls to use for schoolwork with the understanding that they wouldn't use them much for play. But she knew from other mothers that it was extremely difficult to control their children's use of computers, and their policies ranged from not allowing computers in the home to not even trying to control their use. "So they have a website. When we get home I want to see it."

"Okay. But please don't tell them I told you about it."

"Are you afraid of them?"

"No. But they could say things about me."

"You mean on the internet? What could they say?"

"Oh, I don't know. They could say I'm a loser because I failed the test."

They were coming down from the top of the hill at Shonnard Place, and Marika was so upset that she had to steady her hands on the wheel. "You only failed at being a thief. And being a successful thief isn't something to be proud of."

Jessica said nothing.

Marika waited until they had turned onto Roberts Avenue and started up the hill there before saying: "I want to know who those girls are. I want to talk with their parents."

"Please don't do that to me."

"Well, someone's gotta stop those girls. What they're doing is criminal."

"I promise not to do anything with them again, but please don't go after them."

"We'll decide what to do about them," Marika said, slowing for the turn onto Bellevue Avenue, "after we've discussed it with your father."

Frank was already home, sitting at the kitchen table with a can of beer, and with a look of concern he asked: "Where were you?"

"Tell your father where we were," she said to Jessica, who had followed her into the kitchen.

"We were at the police station," Jessica said, resting her hands on the back of a chair.

"Tell him why," Marika prompted her.

"I got caught stealing a baseball from a store on Main Street."

"What the hell?" Frank said, shocked. "Why did you do a thing like that?"

"Tell him," Marika said.

Jessica explained about the club.

With a grimace Frank said: "So in order to get into this club you have to commit a crime and get away with it? Is that correct?"

Jessica nodded.

"Well, why did you want to get into the club?"

"I don't know. I guess I wanted to belong to something."

"You already belong to something. You belong to your family."

"You belong to your school, you belong to your church," Marika said.

"You belong to your dojo," Frank added.

"Yeah, I know, but—" Jessica stopped, looking down at the seat of the chair.

"You felt you needed something else?"

"I guess I did, but I don't know what. And I'm sorry I upset you. I promise not to do it again."

"We don't mind if you upset us," Marika said. "We only mind if you do things that could ruin your life. Do you understand?"

"I think I do."

"Whatever you do," Frank said clearly, "it's not about us. It's about you."

"We love you," Marika said.

"I love you too," Jessica said.

There was a long pause.

"I want to see that website," Frank said.

Looking scared, Jessica said: "Well, I don't want them to find out I told you about it."

"They won't find out. They don't know who looks at their website. So please go and get your computer."

While Jessica was doing that Marika said: "I think we should do something about this club."

"I agree," Frank said. "But I don't know what. I think we'd need a computer expert to find out who they are."

"There's a guy at the college who might be able to help us." She had in mind a faculty member in the computer science department whose name was Mukesh.

After Jessica returned with her computer and set it down on the kitchen table Frank found the site and studied it. "Whoever they are, they're pretty sophisticated. They say they're girls, but they could be anybody."

"You mean they might not be girls?" Jessica said as if she felt betrayed.

"People can pretend to be anything on the internet," Frank said. "So if you don't know them personally, you shouldn't trust them."

"You really shouldn't," Marika said.

The next day she went to the college and found Mukesh in his office with a computer on his desk. He was in his mid-forties with a round face and hair receding from his forehead. He wore silver-rimmed glasses, and he sported a bushy black mustache. She knew him from having served on committees with him.

She sat down in front of his desk, explained the situation, and gave him the address of the website, which he quickly entered into his computer.

"Mm," he said after studying the website.

"What do you see?"

"I see a sophisticated website. Did you say it belongs to a girls club?"

"That's what they told my daughter."

"Well, let's see who it really is," Mukash said, and for the next five minutes or so he did things on this keyboard. Then he said: "It's not a girls club. It's just a guy, and guess what—he lives in Scarsdale."

"Scarsdale?" It was one of the wealthiest suburbs in the county.

"If you want to file a complaint, I can give you information on the guy."

She thought about it, and then said: "I promised my daughter that I wouldn't get her into trouble with him, but can you do anything to stop him from what he's doing?"

"I could send a virus into his website."

"What would that do?"

"It would disable his computer," Mukash said, "at least for a while."

"That sounds fine."

She waited while he did more things on his keyboard, wondering how many girls like Jessica the guy had lured into committing crimes. And it wasn't a guy from the ghetto, it was a guy from a wealthy suburb who must have been completely spoiled by his parents.

"Okay, it's done," Mukash said. "But tell your daughter not to trust anyone on the internet. It's a jungle out there."

"I will. Thanks."

When she got home she told Jessica what she had learned from Mukash, and how he had put the website out of commission. She also conveyed his warning not to trust anyone on the internet, and Jessica seemed to accept it.

ELEVEN

SHE HAD LUNCH on the deck, an egg salad sandwich, and since it was another nice day she lingered there, idly watching the birds and the squirrels. Frank was coming home around three to take her back to the hospital, so she had time to kill until then. She was thankful that Jessica was being released tomorrow, but she knew it would only be the beginning of another round of trying to help Jessica get her life together. Along with her unconditional love she still had a residue of hope, but her faith was challenged, and she prayed for her daughter, prayed for her family, prayed for her community, and prayed for the messed-up world that the doctor said they had given their kids. And her mind went back to what had happened after Jessica found out that the club for girls she tried to join was only a scam.

She had driven Jessica to karate class, and she was watching while Jessica prepared for the event at which she could earn her black belt. After performing the required series of kata, she had a sparring match with a boy. From watching previous classes Marika knew that the boy was a year older than Jessica, and that he had been doing karate since the age of six. He had long limbs, which he moved so gracefully that Marika thought he could have been a dancer. He had earned his black belt last year, and next year he was going away to college.

Like all the sparring in the classes this match was supposed to be friendly. The students were expected to strike at each other but at the same time to restrain themselves from hurting each other. The overriding purpose was to perform the moves according to form while always maintaining self-control. And in this respect the match began well. The boy was good but Marika, possibly biased in favor of her daughter, thought Jessica was just as good, and it was a pleasure to watch them spar.

At one point when Jessica let down her guard the boy landed a sidekick on her hip that knocked her off balance. She quickly recovered, but instead of continuing the match as before she lost control and fought as if she wanted to kill the boy. With a flurry of punches and kicks she drove him to the side of floor and then she aimed a roundhouse kick directly at his groin. The boy partly blocked it, but the impact made him groan in pain, and from his contortions it was clear that he could no longer continue fighting.

"That's enough," Deylin said. "Let's take a break."

Jessica stood there with clenched fists as if she was ready to keep fighting, but Deylin put an arm around her shoulder and guided her over to a chair and made her sit down. He used the last ten minutes of the class to have the students practice some routines, and then he dismissed them. In the meantime the boy, who had sat down a few chairs away from Jessica, seemed to have recovered, and he got up and went over to Jessica.

"That was a good kick," he said, "but I should have blocked it."

"I'm sorry," she said. "I really didn't mean to hurt you."

"It's okay. Don't worry."

When the boy had packed up and gone Deylin came over and said to Jessica: "It's not okay. You lost control. You acted like you wanted to hurt him."

"I'm sorry," Jessica said. "I don't know what happened to me."

"Well, until I'm convinced that you won't ever do that again, you'll have to put off getting your black belt. You'll have to work on controlling yourself."

Jessica nodded as if she accepted his judgment.

As they were driving home Marika asked: "What made you lose control?"

"I don't know," Jessica said glumly. "I guess it was getting kicked in the hip."

"But I've seen you get kicked like that before. Do you have something against that boy?"

"No, I have nothing against him. We spar all the time with no problem. I even like him."

Remembering what had happened two days ago, Marika said:

"Then maybe someone else was on your mind."

"Who do you mean?"

"I mean the guy on the internet who tricked you into thinking he was a girls club."

After a pause Jessica said: "Yeah, maybe. But he wasn't on my mind when I lost control."

"He might not have been at the top of your mind, but he could have been at the bottom of it."

"Yeah, I guess."

"Have you been thinking about him?"

"Yeah."

Marika waited, but when Jessica didn't say anything further she asked: "What have you been thinking about him?"

"I've been thinking I want to kill him," Jessica said without apparent feeling.

"I understand. But killing him wouldn't solve anything. You have to put him behind you and not let him affect your life."

"Okay. I'll stop thinking about him."

"It won't be easy, and it'll take time. But just remember, your father and I are always here for you, so you can talk with us about anything. We love you."

"I know." A long pause. "Do you think I should still go for my black belt?"

"You should do whatever you think is best for you," Marika said. "The black belt isn't for us, it's for you."

"Okay. I'll think about it."

Though Jessica decided not to go for a black belt she continued karate until she started college a year and a half later, and then she no longer had time for it. Jessica wanted to pursue a career in which she could help people, and the two main possibilities that she considered were nursing and teaching. She leaned toward nursing because it involved doing physical things for people, so she applied to the nursing program at St. Catherine, and she was accepted. She started well despite the challenges of anatomy and physiology in her first year and microbiology in her second year, and after three semesters she had a cumulative GPA of 3.7, which was honors level.

Meanwhile Nina was going to high school at Maria Regina, and her main interests were boys and fashion, neither of which she had much exposure to because she went to a girls school where they had to wear uniforms, so most of what she knew about boys and fashion came from watching television. By her junior year she had decided where she wanted to go to college—the Fashion Institute of Technology, which was in the city. The tuition wouldn't be free, as it would be at St. Catherine because as faculty Marika received free tuition for members of her immediate family, but FIT was in the state system so its tuition was relatively low.

That was the year when students began to appear in class with smartphones, which Marika referred to as "monkey toys." Before, when she came into the classroom the lights were on and the students were engaged with each other, sitting or standing or moving around. Now, when she came into the classroom the lights were off and the students were immobile, seated at their desks, engrossed in their monkey toys, oblivious of each other. At one point when a boy did something on his phone while Marika was explaining the difference between two adjectives that an author had used in a story, she asked him to put the phone away, which he did for a while but then he took it out again. She realized that in order to conduct an effective class she would need a strict policy on smartphones, and that evening she discussed the problem with Frank, who proposed a solution.

The next day he went to a sporting goods store in White Plains and purchased a set of yellow and red cards used by soccer referees, which the following day she took to her afternoon class and set on the lectern along with her notes.

"Most of you have smartphones," she told the students, "and I can see how they might be useful for a lot of things, but during class time you are not allowed to use them. If I see you on your phone during class time, I will issue you a yellow card." At that point she held up the yellow card for them to see. "You know what that means?"

"It's a warning," a boy said.

"Right. It's a warning. And if I see you on your phone again, I will issue you a red card." At that point she held up the red card. "You know what that means?"

"It means you're out of the game," the boy said.

"Exactly. You're out of the game. You leave the classroom and you get a zero on your work for that week."

"What happens if you do it again?"

"You fail the course."

"That's not fair," another boy argued. "In baseball you get three strikes."

"This isn't baseball. You're not here to play, you're here to work." She paused for a moment before asking: "How many of you have jobs?"

Almost all the students raised a hand.

"Well, what would your boss do if you pulled out your phone while he was explaining something to you?"

"He'd fire me," a girl said.

"He would for sure," Marika said. "And that's what I'll do if you get two red cards."

They evidently got the message because from then on not one student took out a phone during class time.

Of course the issue of smartphones had come up at home, and there it wasn't about when their children could use them but about whether they should even have them. Marika and Frank had provided Jessica and Nina with cellphones for use in an emergency, but they were opposed to their having smartphones, which at best could distract them from what they should be doing and at worst could get them into trouble. But after weeks of hearing that all the other kids had them Marika and Frank agreed to let their children have smartphones on several conditions that limited their use. And one of these conditions was that at bedtime they would hand the phones over to their parents for the night.

As the months passed it looked as if the phones weren't having any negative effects on their children. From what Marika could observe of their behavior, Jessica used her phone a lot to find answers to questions that she had trouble finding in her textbooks, and Nina used her phone a lot to talk with girlfriends. Both of them were involved in social media but neither of them seemed to have gotten addicted.

By the end of the spring semester Marika wasn't worrying about the phones, and she wasn't anxious about how the girls were doing at school. She was under pressure to submit the grades of her students on time, which she did, and then out of curiosity she checked the system to see how Jessica had done in her courses, expecting A's as usual. She was shocked to see that Jessica had gotten FW's in all her courses, which meant that early in the semester she had stopped attending them.

When she made this discovery she was in the guestroom, which she used as an office, and she gave herself time to calm down before going into Jessica's room, where she found Jessica lying on her bed, holding her phone and gazing at its screen.

"Hey, Jess," Marika said, sitting down on the edge of the bed. "How are you doing?"

"Oh, I'm okay," Jessica said as if she sensed that something was wrong.

"What happened this semester?"

"What do you mean?"

"I just saw your grades."

Jessica sighed.

"You told me things were going well."

"They were, but—"

"Did something happen?"

"No, not really."

"Then why did you stop attending your courses?"

After a long painful silence Jessica said: "I felt I couldn't do them."

"But you did well for three semesters. You even did well on the killer courses like anatomy and physiology. So why did you feel you couldn't do those courses?"

"I don't know. I guess I felt I was a loser."

"You're not a loser," Marika said, knowing that this was a sore point for Jessica.

"Well, I felt like one."

"Where did this come from?"

Jessica said nothing.

"Did it come from the internet?"

Again, Jessica said nothing.

"If it did, please tell me."

"Well, I guess it did. Those girls on the internet have everything, and I have nothing."

"Whoever they are, they're bullshitting. Didn't I tell you not to trust anyone on the internet?"

"But they have pictures of all these things."

"Whatever they're showing you, it's fake. If it was real they wouldn't have to show it to people." Marika paused, hoping that Jessica would understand. "What you have is real, and it's more than they have."

"What do I have?"

"You have the ability to do anything you want to. I mean within reason. You can't flap your arms and fly to the moon."

Jessica almost smiled at that.

"Hey," Marika said, "you had a bad semester, but it's not the end of the world. Everyone has a bad semester."

"I bet you didn't, and I bet Dad didn't."

"We both had bad times, but we got through them. And you'll get through this. But you have to talk with us. If you're having a problem, please don't hide it from us. If we don't know what's happening, we can't help you."

"I know," Jessica said with tears in her eyes.

"We both love you," Marika said, leaning over and hugging her daughter. She didn't know what she was going to do, but she had to do something.

That evening, sitting on the sofa in the living room, Marika and Frank talked about what had happened. One question was whether Jessica should continue the nursing program, and they agreed to let Jessica decide. Another question was what Jessica should do if she decided not to continue the program. But the most important question was how they could help Jessica deal with her problem, whatever it was.

"I think she should talk with someone besides us," Frank said.

"You mean a therapist?"

"Yeah. I don't want her to see a psychiatrist. That could make her feel there's something wrong with her."

"Well, maybe there *is* something wrong with her."

"There's something wrong with all of us."

"Yeah, I know. But there could be something deep inside of her, something that makes her feel inadequate."

"If there is, a therapist could find that out. I don't want some doctor putting her on drugs."

"Oh, I don't either. I just wonder what it is." She paused. "Do you think it's us?"

"What do you mean?"

"Do you think we could have done something to make her feel inadequate?"

"We could have, but what?"

"We could have expected too much from her."

"Yeah, we could have. But it was her idea to go into nursing."

"It was," she agreed. "And she was doing well in the program. So why did she feel she couldn't do those courses?"

"I don't know. But I don't think it was something we did."

"Well, I feel it was something I did."

"Why do you feel that?"

"Because I'm her mother."

"Yeah, you're her mother," he said calmly, "but that doesn't make you responsible for everything that happens to her."

"I know. But I can't help feeling it does."

He put an arm around her shoulder acknowledging her feeling, and after a silence he said: "So let's talk with her."

She got up from the sofa and went to the bottom of the stairs and called up to Jessica, who didn't take long to respond. It was as if she was waiting for them to call her.

"We've been talking about what happened," Marika told her, "and we'd like to talk with you about it. Okay?"

"Okay," Jessica said, dropping heavily into an easy chair.

"Do you want to continue the nursing program?"

"Yeah, I do. But not this fall. I'd like to wait until next spring."

"That's fine. So what do you want to do in the meantime?"

"I want to work in a hospital so I can find out what it's like."

"That sounds like a good idea," Frank said. "What would you do in a hospital?"

"Well, I could work as a nursing assistant."

"That makes sense. It would give you experience for being a nurse if that's what you decide to be."

"If you want to be a nursing assistant," Marika said, "you'll have to take a program for that and get certified."

"Do they have a program at St. Catherine?" Frank asked.

"No, but they have a program at Cochran School of Nursing, so Jess should find out about that program."

"Okay. I will," Jessica said.

After a pause Marika said: "We're also wondering if you want to talk with a therapist."

"What would we talk about?" Jessica said uneasily.

"Anything you want to talk about."

"Well, I don't see how that could help."

"It could help you understand yourself better."

Jessica looked doubtful, as if she might not want to understand herself better.

"It would give you a different perspective," Frank said. "And that could be helpful."

Jessica considered. "Would the therapist tell you what we talked about?"

"Only if you gave her your permission," Marika told her.

"It would be a woman?" Jessica said, brightening.

"I think it should be," Frank said. "Unless you want a man."

"No, I don't want a man. I want a woman."

"Then if it's okay with you," Marika said, "we'll look for a therapist."

"Yeah, it's okay with me," Jessica said.

Marika knew from her colleagues in the psychology department that some of their instructors had practices and taught part time, so she asked the chairperson if she could recommend a therapist, ideally someone who worked with young women. The chairperson gave her three candidates, and after checking their resumés Marika selected a therapist named Ellen Bernstein who had a practice in Hastings. She made an appointment, and later that week she drove Jessica to the therapist's office, which was in a building on North Broadway.

There was no receptionist but after a moment a dark-haired woman in her mid-forties appeared from an inner room, and they exchanged introductions in which the woman asked them to call her Ellen. They went into the inner room, where they got acquainted by talking about their associations with St. Catherine. Then Ellen got down to business and asked Jessica a series of questions to establish background, making notes on a clipboard. When that was done she asked Marika if she would wait in the outer room while she talked one-on-one with Jessica.

After almost an hour, during which Marika killed time by thumbing through magazines, the door to the inner room opened and Ellen invited her to join them.

"Jessica and I have agreed to meet twice a week for at least a while," Ellen told her. "We'll see how it goes, and if it's going well then we can meet only once a week. Is that okay?"

"Yes, it's okay," Marika said.

"Jessica has given me permission to share with you what we talk about, so I'll meet with you once a month to review our progress. Okay?"

"Okay."

They talked for a while and ended by making a schedule of appointments for Jessica, and then they thanked Ellen and left.

As they drove home Jessica said: "I like her."

"Good. And based on what I saw of her, I like her too."

"She didn't give me any bullshit."

Marika couldn't help smiling. "I hope that doesn't mean I give you bullshit."

"Oh, no, you don't. And Dad doesn't either. But some of the teachers at the college do."

Though curious, she refrained from asking who they were.

After a silence Jessica said: "We talked about why I stopped attending my courses this spring, and she asked if I could have been sending a message."

"What kind of message?"

"That I didn't want to be in the program."

Open to that possibility, Marika asked: "What did you tell her?"

"I told her I didn't know, I'd have to think about it."

"Well, just remember, your father and I will support whatever you want to do. And if you want to help people, nursing isn't the only way."

"Yeah, I know. But I want to work as a nursing assistant before I make any decision."

"So call Cochran and make an appointment."

When they got home Jessica called Cochran, and the next day Marika drove her there. The nursing school was attached to St. John's Hospital, and after parking the car they found the door that led into the school. They had a productive meeting with the woman in charge of admissions who described the program and told them there might still be room for Jessica in the class that began in September. They left it that Jessica would have a decision as soon as the school had reviewed her transcripts.

Two weeks later Jessica received a letter informing her that she had been admitted to the nursing assistant program at Cochran, so Jessica could go ahead and tell the college that she would be taking a semester off.

That summer Marika found a woman who taught at the high school in Hastings to give Jessica driver's lessons because the courses in the nursing assistant program were in the evening, and though Cochran was in walking distance from their house they didn't want her walking home at night, and Jessica didn't want them to have to pick her up after class. So in early June she began taking driving lessons, which went well. The woman was patient and kind, and Jessica readily learned from her.

Meanwhile Jessica had met with the therapist several times, and Marika was invited to meet with her and get a review. She sat on the sofa in Ellen's office, and Ellen sat in a swivel chair. They chatted for a while, and then Ellen said: "Well, I've picked up some things from my conversations with Jessica, and one thing that stands out is that she has a strong aversion to guys. Were you aware of it?"

"Oh, yeah. She doesn't like guys."

"I can understand why. I mean, young guys are mostly drippy. And before the age of twelve or so I didn't like them either. But with Jessica I have the feeling it's more than the usual aversion. Did a guy ever hurt her?"

Marika nodded, remembering. "When she was in elementary school a guy called her a loser."

"How did she react?'

"She hit him and gave him a black eye."

"Well, that's another thing I picked up. She's very aggressive."

"Yeah, I know. We had her take karate classes so she could learn to control her aggression."

"What a great idea," Ellen said. "Did it help her?"

"It got her almost through high school. But when she was going for her black belt she lost control and hurt the guy she was sparring with."

"Did she have something against the guy?"

"No. She had something against another guy. But it's more than that. I mean, she has something against guys."

"Do you have any idea why?"

Marika shook her head. "I have no idea."

"Was she abused by an uncle or a teacher?"

"No, not that I know of. She only has one uncle, her father's younger brother, and until she went to college she never had a male teacher."

"What about a priest?"

"The only priests she ever knew were at our church. They weren't teachers in her schools, and they weren't involved in her religious education."

"So we can rule out her being abused by an older man?"

"I think we can," Marika said.

"Then it's something deeper." Ellen paused, reflecting. "What kind of relationship does she have with her father?"

"She has a good relationship with him, and she has a good relationship with her grandfather."

"So she doesn't have a problem with older men."

"No, she doesn't. She has a problem with guys her age."

"Okay. Do you remember anything else that a guy did to her?"

"Yeah. When she was a junior in high school a guy on the internet tricked her into believing he was a girls club."

"A girls club?" Ellen repeated with interest. "What exactly did he do to her?"

"He got her to steal a baseball from a sporting goods store in downtown Yonkers."

"How did he get her to do that?"

"He made it a condition for her to get into the club."

"Did she get caught stealing the baseball?"

"Yeah, she got caught, and she was angry when she found out that the girls club was a guy."

"Of course she was," Ellen said as if she understood. "So did she do anything to get back at him?"

"Not directly, but I think she got back at him indirectly by hurting that guy she was sparring with."

Ellen was silent for a while thinking, and then she asked: "Do you understand why she wanted to get into that girls club?"

"I think I do," Marika said. "She likes girls."

"That's the other thing I picked up. Are you okay with that?"

"Sure. I don't care who she likes. I just want her to be happy."

"The strange thing is, she didn't mention any girlfriends. Does she have girlfriends?"

"She had girlfriends in high school, but I haven't heard about any in college."

"Well, maybe she was working so hard to do well in the nursing program that she didn't have time for girlfriends. And maybe that's why she stopped attending those courses."

Marika considered. "So you think she stopped attending those courses because they didn't give her time for girlfriends?"

"It's a possibility," Ellen said. "I don't know why she stopped attending those courses, but whatever the reason was, she did it deliberately."

"Okay. But she hasn't given up the idea of being a nurse."

"I know. She told me she just enrolled in a nursing assistant program so she can find out what it's like being a nurse. That's a rational course of action, and if she does well in the program, it could restore her self-confidence."

"But how did she lose her self-confidence?" Marika asked. "She was doing so well."

"It happens to people. On the surface they seem okay, but at a deeper level something is festering, growing like a tumor, and bang, it bursts out."

"And you have no idea what it was?"

"I'm only a therapist," Ellen said. "I'm not God."

"Then how can you help her?"

"I can help her change the negative thoughts and behaviors that get her into trouble. I can help her learn better ways of coping. But I can only help her if she wants to be helped. If she doesn't, then nothing will happen."

"I understand," Marika said.

Jessica did well in the nursing assistant program. She finished as one of the top five students and was offered a job at St. John's Hospital. By then she had passed the tests for a driver's license so they found a used Honda Civic for her, which Marika's father checked for problems that the seller didn't divulge or didn't know about, and with his approval they bought it. Jessica agreed to use the car only to get to work and come home.

In January she started working full time as a nursing assistant, and she did well at the job, doing things that most people wouldn't do. Her manager gave her very good evaluations, and her patients appreciated her. In the meantime Marika didn't raise the question of when or whether Jessica would go back to college. She realized that Jessica was fully engaged by her job, so she waited for Jessica to raise the question, which she finally did.

"I think I'll go back to college this fall," Jessica said one evening while they were in the kitchen preparing dinner.

"Okay," Marika said, stirring the sauce for the pasta.

"But I'm going to change my major."

"Okay." Students frequently changed their majors, so it was no big deal.

"I like working in the hospital, but from what I've seen there I don't want to be a nurse."

"What do you want to be?"

"I want to be someone who helps people with mental problems."

Presumably she had been influenced by her relationship with Ellen. "You mean a therapist?"

"Yeah. So I think I should change my major to psychology."

"Well, that would be the appropriate major."

"And since I have a full-time job, I think I should be a part-time student. What do you think?"

"I think it's a good idea," Marika said, "at least until you find out what it's like going to college and working full time."

"You have students who do that, don't you?"

"Of course. Some work full time and go to college part time, while others work part time and go to college full time. The thing is to get the right balance between college and work."

"Do any of them work full time and go to college full time?"

"Oh, yeah. But they're usually older. They've been working for a while after stopping college. and they've come back wanting to finish as soon as possible."

"Well, I'm not in a hurry to finish."

"You shouldn't be. So try to find what works for you."

That fall Jessica went back to college as a psychology major, taking two courses per semester, so she was working at the hospital five days a week and going to classes two evenings a week, and she was staying out of trouble. By then Marika was worrying more about Nina, who had started going to FIT and was living in a dorm there with a girl who sounded crazy. The college had assigned this roommate to her, and while Nina liked her she didn't like being under pressure from her to do things at night that she knew her parents wouldn't approve of. It wasn't that she was against meeting guys in bars, but she didn't like the kind of guys that her roommate was attracted to. So she started coming home most weekends. During that time Nina and Jessica became closer, which Marika was delighted to see. What made her laugh was overhearing Jessica counsel her sister, telling her how to handle the situation with her roommate. It was as if Jessica was already practicing as a therapist.

Everything was going well until the spring semester of the following year when around eleven on a Friday night Marika got a phone call from a girl who told her she had just dropped Jessica off at the emergency room of St. John's Hospital. The girl refused to give her name and abruptly hung up before Marika could ask any questions.

She roused Frank from watching the news, and they drove to the hospital only able to speculate about what had happened. The woman at the reception desk of the ER told them Jessica was at that moment being treated by a doctor, whom she contacted to let him know they were there. So along with other anxious people they sat down in the waiting area, where Marika closed her eyes and prayed. They waited for a long time before a doctor appeared and informed them that Jessica was all right but had suffered head wounds from a fight. He didn't think she had a concussion, but he was still testing to rule that out.

He led them to the bed where Jessica was stretched out with a prominent bandage on her face. In her eyes was a look of utter hopelessness.

"The doctor says you're all right," Marika told her, taking a listless hand. "Thank God."

"How do you feel?" Frank asked her.

"I feel like shit," Jessica said.

"Do you have a headache?"

"Yeah. And it hurts where he hit me in the face."

"Who hit you?"

"A guy outside a bar."

"What bar?"

"Oh, I don't remember the name of it. We didn't stay there very long."

"But long enough to get into a fight."

"Yeah. Well, he started it."

"How did he start it?"

"He called me a lesbian loser."

"Oh, Jess," Marika said feeling bad for her. "Why did you care what some guy called you?"

"It hurt me, that's why. So I wanted to hurt him back."

"You should have walked away from him," Frank told her.

"Yeah, I know. But I just couldn't. I tried to kick him in the balls, but I missed, and he grabbed my foot and took me down."

"He hit you when you were down?"

"Yeah. He also kicked me."

"So he's a loser, but you started the physical fight."

Jessica sighed. "I know. And I'm sorry."

"Where was the bar?" Marika asked.

"On McClean Avenue."

"What were you doing there?"

"I went there with a friend."

"You mean the girl who brought you here? What's her name?"

"It doesn't matter. I don't ever want to see her again."

"Did something go wrong between you?"

"No. She just wasn't what she said she was."

"Did you meet her on the internet?"

"Yeah, I did. There's nowhere else to meet people."

It was the same pattern in which Jessica kept getting off the rotary at the wrong exit, and though Marika hoped and prayed for her she didn't see how everything could fall into place, as Father Paul had said it would.

TWELVE

ON FRIDAY SINCE Jessica was being released from the hospital
later that morning Marika drove down to Jessica's apartment to
get clothes and other things she would need while she was back
living at home. The apartment was in one of the many high-rise
buildings in Greystone built in recent years, right on the bank of
the Hudson River, south of Hastings.

Marika had a key from Jessica, but for good order she informed
the woman at the desk in the lobby that she was going into the
apartment. The woman evidently didn't know that Jessica hadn't
been there for the past week, and Marika let her know that Jessica
would be away for a while. The apartment was around the corner
from the lobby, and Marika let herself in. It was a spacious studio,
which she had helped Jessica furnish. To conserve space they had
bought a sofa bed, which in theory would be folded up during the
day, but it was down, and on the bed was a tangle of sheets, which
upon closer inspection hadn't been changed in a long time. The
floor was littered with items of clothing, including dirty underwear,
as well as not quite empty containers of take-out food, plastic cups,
and beer bottles.

The kitchen was also a mess. There were unwashed plates in
the sink and a bottle of ketchup on the counter along with several
empty cans. There were only a few items inside the refrigerator,
including a container of leftover food that was growing green mold
and a carton of spoiled milk.

Resisting a voice in her head that told her she was only enabling
Jessica, she spent the next hour cleaning up the apartment. And
when she was done she stripped the bed of the dirty sheets and
stuffed them into a laundry bag, which she set against the door so
she wouldn't forget to take it with her.

At that point she went out to the patio and found a bench, where she sat down and gazed at the river, wondering what she had done wrong. Almost seven years ago Jessica had completed a bachelor's degree in psychology, but she was still working as a nursing assistant at St. John's hospital. With no more homework to do she had more time to spend on her smartphone, and from what she revealed about her activities Marika believed that she was avidly searching on the internet for someone who would fill the void in her heart and make her happy.

In the meantime Nina had completed her program at FIT after living off-campus for her last two years, sharing an apartment in the West 130's with two compatible female classmates, and now she had a job with a fashion magazine and was living in the West 80's with a guy who was an associate at a law firm. They were both working so hard they barely had time for each other, but that was all right with Nina, who as much as she liked the guy wasn't yet ready to make a commitment.

On her income as a nursing assistant Jessica couldn't afford to rent her own apartment. The only way was to share an apartment, and even though she had friends among her colleagues at the hospital they all either had boyfriends or were looking for boyfriends, and that made them ineligible. So she had still been living at home and staying out of trouble.

Then one afternoon that fall Marika got a phone call from Jessica, who said she needed a ride home because she had gotten into an accident with her car. The location was in Dobbs Ferry, so it didn't take long for Marika to get there. When she arrived she saw the flashing lights of a police car and a tow truck getting into position to remove Jessica's car. They were at the intersection of Route 9 and Livingston Avenue, which led into the commercial area. After parking her car Marika approached Jessica, who was talking with a police officer and a guy with a shaved head and tattooed arms.

"I don't care what that bitch says," the guy said, "she rammed into me deliberately."

"I didn't," Jessica argued back. "You stopped suddenly with no warning."

"I stopped because the light was red."

"It wasn't red. It wasn't even yellow when you stopped."

"I hear you both," the officer said, "and I believe it was an accident. So clear this scene."

It took them a few more minutes to disengage, and then Jessica went along with Marika and got into the car.

"What really happened?" Marika asked as they drove away.

"He cut me off," Jessica said. "He almost drove me off the road. so I went after him."

"And rammed into him deliberately?"

"Yeah. But he had it coming. People like him shouldn't be allowed to drive."

"You're probably right, but it's not your job to deal with the problem. And you could have been injured."

"I know. I'm sorry."

"Also, you lied to the police officer."

"I had to lie. Did you want me to get arrested?"

"No. But I didn't want you to ram that guy."

"I'm sorry," Jessica said. "But I just couldn't help it."

"You should talk with Ellen," Marika told her. "Make an appointment with her, okay?"

"Okay. I will. I'll pay for the damage."

"Your insurance should cover it. But they'll probably raise your premium."

Jessica let out a long sigh as if that was the worst thing about what had happened.

Over the next year Jessica met people on the internet who needed money to deal with a variety of problems. Among others there was one in Los Angeles, one in Las Vegas, and one in Phoenix. They were all women, or pretending to be women, and they all convinced Jessica that they were in love with her, so she gave them money amounting to thousands of dollars. Marika wouldn't have known about it if Frank hadn't spotted unusual payments in her bank statements while reviewing them to prepare her taxes. When they asked Jessica about the payments she was evasive, but eventually she admitted what she had been doing.

"You're paying a lot of money to those people," Frank said as they discussed it, sitting in the living room, "and you don't even know them."

"I thought I knew them," Jessica said.

"But you never met them in person, so how could you tell if they were who they claimed to be?"

"I believed they were, and I wanted to help them."

"If you want to help people by giving them money," Marika said gently, "give it to Catholic Charities, but don't give it to people you meet on the internet."

"Those people make a living by preying on the generosity of others," Frank said.

"Well, I thought they loved me."

"If you want love," Marika said, "you're looking in the wrong place. There are real people all around you who love you."

"Starting with us," Frank said.

"Yeah, I know."

After a silence Marika asked: "Have you talked with Ellen about this?"

"Oh, yeah. And she says the same thing you do. She also says I shouldn't be looking for someone to make me happy, I should learn to make myself happy."

"I agree with her."

"But I don't know how to make myself happy."

"You're helping people at the hospital," Frank said. "Doesn't that make you happy?"

"Yeah. But it's not enough."

"So maybe you need to find a way to help people more."

"I've thought about that," Jessica said. "And I think I could help people more as a teacher."

"When you first went to college," Marika said, "you wanted to be a nurse or a teacher."

"Yeah, I know. But I'd need a master's in education to be a teacher, and I'm not ready to go back to school yet."

"That's okay. But in the meantime don't give money to people you meet on the internet. At least get involved with a real person."

Jessica agreed to stop getting involved with people she met on the internet, and Ellen put her into group therapy with five other young women who were struggling with issues of gender identity. They met once a week in Ellen's office, on Thursday evenings, and with Ellen moderating they shared their problems and acted as a support group for each other. Jessica liked all the members of the group, but she didn't fall in love with any of them.

Several months later she did fall in love with someone, and this time it was a real person, a young woman named Lola who worked as a clerk at the hospital. They started dating, going out to dinner on weekends and hanging out at Lola's apartment. Lola was an immigrant from El Salvador who had come to New York with her parents at the age of eight. After a while Jessica invited Lola for dinner and introduced her. She was attractive, well dressed, and well mannered. Marika and Frank both liked her, and they were glad that Jessica had finally found a real person to have a relationship with.

A week later Jessica announced that she was going to move in with Lola, whose previous roommate had left the area for another job. Marika had mixed feelings about this, and she called Ellen to get her opinion. Ellen said there were risks but Jessica would never learn anything if she didn't take risks and make mistakes, so her advice was to let Jessica go and do it. In any case Jessica, at twenty-nine, was old enough to do what she wanted.

The relationship lasted more than a year. It ended when Lola allowed a guy to come home with her and sleep with her. Since Jessica had been operating on the assumption that Lola only liked women, she felt betrayed, and in the kitchen she threw a plate at the guy, who came after her, only to find that he was dealing with someone who had a brown belt in karate. Jessica landed some kicks and punches, but the guy eventually overwhelmed her, and she ended up in the emergency room. Marika drove her home from the hospital, feeling her pain as she sobbed her heart out, doubled up on the passenger's seat.

During that summer Jessica applied to St. Catherine for the master's program in early childhood education, and based on her undergraduate record she was accepted. She began the program that fall while still working full time as a nursing assistant. She pointed out that since she didn't have much of a social life she would be able to work full time and go to college full time. She registered for three courses, and she got A's in all of them.

In the meantime Marika's father had moved out of his house and into assisted living at Meadowview, which was on the campus of Wartburg in Mt. Vernon. It had started with his falling off a ladder while trimming a hedge and breaking his femur. After surgery the doctor sent him to Wartburg for rehabilitation, and while he was there Marika noticed that they had facilities for assisted living. It had taken a while for her to convince him to leave his house and go to Meadowview, but he had finally gone along with it after meeting the director of Meadowview, a pretty woman in her mid-thirties whose name was Kathleen. Marika had gotten him a deluxe studio on the main floor, right around the corner from Kathleen's office, so he could easily get her attention.

It worked out well. Her father reverted to a period of his life when he was a socially active young man, and it wasn't long before everyone at Meadowview knew him, including the Dominican girls who served the meals and the staff who took their breaks on the terrace, where in the good weather he sat on a bench and smoked a cigar while reading the *Daily News*. He also became buddies with a guy named Sal who had served in the army during World War II and had owned a landscaping business. Together they formed a group to play poker every night after dinner. Marika still had him to dinner or took him out on Saturdays, but at other times she had a feeling that he had such a busy social life he had to work her into his schedule.

With her father settled Marika began the painful process of selling his house. She found an agent on Palisade Avenue who was very helpful, telling her what she had to do in preparation for the sale and who could help her dispose of things she didn't want. She had already moved the furniture that would fit into her father's apartment, and there weren't many things that she could use, but it was hard to get rid of things that had been in the family for so long. She asked Julia to help her, but Julia was busy making money, so she and Frank, with help from their daughters, cleared out the house. Among the things she didn't part with were a Polish flag and a picture of the Polish pope.

It only took about three months to sell the house. She got a very good price for it, and she deposited the money into her father's bank account. From there it went into government bonds that provided income in addition to his pension and his social security to pay for Meadowview. There was enough, though she and Frank were prepared to make up any shortfall.

In February everything changed with the arrival of covid. Marika, who read the *New York Times* every morning online, was aware of the novel virus but she first encountered it when a student in ENGL112 told her she wasn't feeling well. As usual, Marika advised the girl to go directly home and lie down and drink plenty of water, but she sensed that the girl didn't have the usual flu or whatever was going around, and she dismissed the class after telling them to check their email to see if the next class would meet in person. Years ago she had flipped her classes by putting all the work online that didn't have to be done in a classroom, so unlike most of the other faculty she was prepared to offer her courses entirely online.

The next day, while waiting for the college to make a decision, she emailed her students that until further notice they would stop meeting in person for her classes. Two weeks later the college decided not to continue having students meet in person for classes and to start training faculty to teach entirely online. Of course Marika was asked to lead the team that would train faculty in their department to teach online, which more than doubled her workload.

Her primary concern was for her family. Frank's company enabled its employees to work remotely, as did Nina's and Julia's companies, so they were relatively safe. The most vulnerable were her father and Jessica. Her father was in a situation that was especially at risk for covid, which was killing many people in facilities for senior citizens, and Jessica was in a hospital where covid patients were being sent. To deal with her father's situation she drove over to Meadowview and invited him to come and live with her for the duration, but her father wouldn't hear of it. He said he had lived a good life, and whatever time he had left he preferred to spend at Meadowview with his buddy Sal. Though he didn't mention it he probably also wanted to be where he could compliment Kathleen on her clothes and her hair.

Jessica dealt with her situation by moving into a motel in Ardsley on the Saw Mill River Road. She said that the hospital was being taken over by covid patients, and she didn't want to bring the virus home and give it to her parents. She had a special rate at the motel, but it still cost too much money, and they decided that Jessica should find an apartment. After all, she was thirty-one, and she was overdue to have her own place.

It took them a month to find an apartment, a studio in one of the multilevel buildings that had sprouted up along the river in an area called Greystone. The location was ideal because it was five minutes from the hospital and the college. The apartment was on the main floor, with glass doors leading out to a patio and beyond to a terrace and a swimming pool. The rent wasn't a bargain but it was a lot less than paying for the motel. Still, it was more than Jessica could afford, so Marika agreed to pay a thousand dollars of it, which left Jessica with enough money for her daily needs. Marika wished she had some of the furniture that she had disposed of from her father's house, but she found a sofa bed, a bureau, and a desk at a store on Tuckahoe Road, which she bought for Jessica. So Jessica moved into the apartment.

Meanwhile, they were adapting to covid. The local supermarket had been stripped by hoarders of things like toilet paper, bread, pasta, tuna, and cleaning products. The hardest thing to find was toilet paper, so Marika searched on Amazon and settled for a dozen rolls of commercial toilet paper, a roll of which according to Frank would stretch from their house to Roberts Avenue. To deal with the shortage of bread she bought twenty pounds of flour and learned how to bake bread. Eventually she was able to buy most of the other things on the internet except for fresh fruits and vegetables, which in theory were available at Whole Foods but for quite a while there were no windows of delivery available. She could only get them by going to the local supermarket early in the morning before the hoarders got them all.

Of course they wore masks everywhere, and even those weren't easy to get. For some reason they were only made in China or other foreign countries, so Marika made them, using pieces of bedsheet and sewing them by hand. At least she finally found a use for the sewing lessons her mother had given her.

Then there was church, which was closed for the duration. Luckily, their parish had a few techies who enabled Father Paul to stream the Masses, and that worked well, though it wasn't possible to take communion virtually. In checking with her father she was glad to learn that he was able to take communion from a priest who visited the facility. She was also relieved to hear that so far there hadn't been any cases of covid at Meadowview.

Meanwhile, the hospital was almost entirely dedicated to treating covid patients, and Jessica was wrapping bodies every day and taking them to the morgue. Marika prayed without ceasing that her daughter wouldn't get covid.

Despite all the disruptions from covid Jessica got A's in her courses that spring, so she now had eighteen credits toward her master's degree.

In September Marika got a phone call from Kathleen who said that her father had been taken to Lawrence Hospital that morning with a respiratory problem. Kathleen didn't think it was covid, she thought it was a longtime problem, but she didn't know. In any case, to be on the safe side the doctor sent him to the hospital.

Marika immediately dropped everything and drove to the hospital, where she found her father lying on a bed with lines attached to him. When she arrived he was dozing, but he soon woke up and asked her: "What am I doing here?"

"The doctor decided you should be here. Apparently you have a respiratory problem."

"What the hell does he know. He's just trying to cover his ass."

"So how do you feel?"

"I feel fine."

"Do you have any problem breathing?"

"No." He took a deep breath as if to prove that he was fine.

"They'll probably keep you here overnight to make sure there's nothing wrong."

Her father scowled. "Then I'll miss the poker game."

"Yeah, you will, but you might have lost money."

"I never lose at poker."

"You lost a few times to Jessica," she reminded him with a quick smile.

"Well, she was lucky." He paused for a moment. "How is she?"

"She's fine. She's busy at the hospital."

"She should find something else to do. She could catch this virus working at the hospital."

"Yeah, she could," Marika said, "so I worry about her."

"And I could catch it being here. Can you get me out of here?"

"I'll talk with the doctor and see what I can do."

"You know," he told her, "you're the one I always rely on, *moja Polska dziewczynka.*"

"*Kocham Cię,*" she said, covering his hand.

"*Ja też cię kocham.*"

She went and found the doctor, who didn't want to release her father. He told her that if her father was all right in the morning he would release him then. Her father wasn't happy about having to spend a night in the hospital, but he accepted it, asking her to come the next morning and take him back to Meadowview.

She left him after kissing his forehead.

The next morning the doctor called her and told her that her father had died during the night, evidently of heart failure.

Under the conditions of covid it was hard to organize the funeral, but she managed to do it over the phone with the Polish funeral home. Since only the immediate family would attend, St. Casimir made a chapel available for the funeral. Besides her, there was only Frank and Jessica and Nina and Julia, together for the first time since before covid. They went in two cars from the church to the cemetery, Julia riding with her and Frank, and Nina riding with Jessica. The one who seemed to take it the hardest was Jessica, which didn't surprise Marika because her father and Jessica always had a special relationship.

For lunch they went to the Portuguese restaurant near the carpet factory, where they could eat safely outside on the terrace. They lingered at the table over glasses of wine, recounting stories about grampa and keeping him alive in their hearts.

That night in bed, with Frank beside her, Marika finally let it all out and drenched the pillow with her tears.

Despite everything that had happened that fall Jessica did well in her courses, getting all A's, and she only had to get through one more semester to complete her master's degree. By then covid vaccines were available, and though it wasn't easy to schedule appointments Marika made sure that every member of her family got vaccinated.

In the spring semester the college tentatively offered a few in-person classes, and Marika taught one of them in addition to her four online courses, but instead of the usual thirty students only seven signed up, indicating that the students had a greater sense of caution than the college administration. Marika wasn't surprised because the students were from groups who lived in densely populated urban neighborhoods and suffered disproportionately from the pandemic. Almost all her students lost their jobs, and many lost family members to covid. Several died after giving her notice that they had covid and needed extra time to submit their assignments. That semester a higher number than usual of Marika's students stopped attending and didn't respond to her email messages offering to help them, and a higher number than usual failed her courses. Still, she was shocked when she saw that Jessica had gotten FW's in all three of her courses.

When she got home with Jessica's things from the apartment she had time to take the laundry bag to the basement and put the dirty sheets into the washer. She could have left it for later, but she had a strong habit of not putting off things she didn't feel like doing, and she carried the clothes up to Jessica's room, where she laid them on the bed and picked out the jeans and top that she thought Jessica would want to wear today. Since Jessica hadn't been living in the room it was neat and clean, and Marika had to accept the fact that it wouldn't be that way for long after Jessica moved back in.

She was standing with the clothes in her arms when Frank appeared in the doorway.

"Did you get everything?" he asked her.

"Yeah, for now. I can always go back later."

"How was the apartment?"

"It was a mess."

"I hope you didn't clean it up."

"You know I did," she said, smiling.

"Well, if she makes a mess of this room," he said, "I hope you don't clean it up."

"I'll try not to, but you know me."

"I do know you," he said, advancing toward her and putting his arms around her. "And I love you. I wouldn't want you to be any other way."

They hugged each other, giving each other the courage they would both need with Jessica in the days ahead.

Before leaving to go and pick up Jessica at the hospital Marika checked the mail. It was only catalogs and promotions, except for a letter from Poland. She had kept up with Maggie, who had gone home after completing her degree and become a high school teacher. That had been more than thirty years ago, and in the meantime Maggie had gotten married and had two children, a boy and a girl, who were now twenty and eighteen.

Going back into the house, Marika put the junk mail on a table in the hall and opened the letter. She was glad to hear that everything was going well for Maggie, and she was delighted to see a photo of Maggie's daughter wearing a traditional Polish dance costume. She kissed the photo and showed it to Frank, who smiled and said: "She looks a lot like Maggie."

"Yeah, she does. Maggie was around that age when I met her."

"What's her daughter's name?"

"Lilka," she said, remembering it from previous letters.

"A pretty name for a pretty girl."

She put the letter with the photo on the table and followed Frank out the door.

When they arrived at the hospital Jessica was still in a patient gown. Marika gave her the clothes she had brought and retired with Frank to the waiting area while Jessica got dressed. Then after a brief meeting with the doctor they left the hospital.

At home Jessica went straight to her room as if to make sure that no one had taken it over in her absence, and then she returned and sat out on the deck, where the three of them eventually had lunch of ham and cheese sandwiches. It was Jessica who raised the subject by saying: "The doctor said I took fentanyl, but I don't remember taking it."

"Do you remember who you were with?" Frank asked.

"I was with a girl I met on the internet, but I don't remember much about her."

"Do you remember her name?"

"No. But even if I did, it wouldn't be her real name."

"Did you give her your real name?"

"Oh, no. I never use my real name in those situations."

"What situations?" Marika asked.

"You know, when I meet someone on the internet. I never tell them my real name or where I live."

"That's good," Frank said as if he was hoping to find something good about it.

"So they'll probably never catch her," Marika said.

"Well, I wish I could help them catch her," Jessica said. "I mean she could be doing the same thing to other girls."

"Yeah, she could be," Frank said.

"So we need to talk about you meeting people on the internet," Marika said. "Not now, but while you're recovering. The next time you might not be so lucky."

"I know," Jessica said solemnly. "And I'm sorry I put you through all that."

Marika believed that Jessica really was sorry, and that was a good sign, but she wondered if that feeling would be translated into action.

Jessica took a medical leave of absence from her job for three weeks, and during the second week Julia called and proposed that she come there on Saturday and bring someone she wanted them to meet. Marika, who hadn't seen her sister since their father's funeral, warmly welcomed the proposal and told Julia she would pick them up at the Yonkers train station.

She took Jessica with her in the car, and they waited on the platform for the train to arrive, wondering who Julia was bringing with her. Jessica, who didn't know Julia very well, said it was probably a boyfriend, but Marika said she wasn't sure. When the train arrived she didn't see Julia at first, but then she saw two women walking toward them from the last car.

As they got closer she could see that the other women was in her fifties with blond hair that was turning silver in a lovely way and serene blue eyes.

"This is Clare," Julia said, introducing her.

Marika took her outstretched hand, saying: "I'm Marika. It's nice to meet you."

Jessica, who was fascinated by the situation, quickly introduced herself and walked ahead as they left the platform.

On the way home Julia asked Marika to drive by the house on Chase Avenue where they had lived so she could show it to Clare, and with commentary from Julia they went up North Broadway to Morsemere Avenue, where they turned and headed toward the house. Clare asked questions, and Julia responded with bits of the family history.

It was a nice day, so Marika planned to sit on the deck and have lunch there. She had poached a large piece of wild salmon and made dill mayonnaise to go with it, together with a green salad and slices of baguette that she had made. She had two bottles of white wine in the refrigerator, ready for consumption. Before serving lunch Marika poured them all a glass of wine, and she listened to Julia talk about Clare and not about herself.

"Clare is the principal of an elementary school in the South Bronx," Julia said. "As you know, it's a poor area, and she does a lot for the kids there."

"That's great," Marika said, seeing the possible implications for Jessica. "How long have you been there?"

"About eight years," Clare said. "Before that I was assistant principal at another elementary school in the area."

"She has her degrees from Columbia," Julia said proudly.

"Where are you from?"

"Buffalo."

By then Marika had noticed that Julia and Clare had matching emerald rings on the fourth fingers of their left hands.

"What's it like at your school?" Jessica asked.

"It's challenging," Clare said, "but it's very rewarding. Julia said you completed a master's in early childhood education."

"I didn't complete it, but I almost did."

"She has one more semester," Marika said, avoiding what had happened the past spring.

"Julia said you teach English at St. Catherine College."

"Yeah. I started teaching there as an adjunct right after we moved here, and it turned out fine. From here I can walk to the college."

"Are you doing classes in-person again?"

"We're doing a few, but most of our students prefer online."

"We did our classes online for a while, and it really hurt our kids. It set them back, and they were already behind the kids who live in affluent neighborhoods."

"I understand," Marika said.

"Kids need personal contact with their teachers."

After they had talked for a while Marika got up and went into the kitchen to bring the food. Jessica helped her, and they continued talking while they ate and drank more wine.

When they had finished lunch Clare asked Jessica to take a walk with her and show her around the neighborhood, leaving Marika and Julia together on the deck.

"What do you think of her?" Julia asked when they were alone.

"I like her," Marika said. "I noticed that you both have rings. Are you engaged?"

"Yeah. We're planning to get married this fall."

"How long have you known her?"

"Almost four years."

"So why haven't I heard about her before?"

With a wry face Julia said: "I think you know why."

"You think Dad wouldn't have approved of the relationship?"

"I know he wouldn't have. I mean, he wasn't homophobic, but he was very traditional."

"I think you underestimate his ability to adapt to things. But that's okay. He can see you from heaven, and he approves of it."

"You believe he's in heaven?"

"Of course he is," Marika said. "Our father was a good man and a good Catholic."

"Clare's Irish, so she was raised as a Catholic."

"What do her parents think about the relationship?"

"They're okay with it. They would have preferred her to marry a man, but they already have five grandchildren, so they don't need her to produce more."

"Well, what about you? Are you still making a lot of money?"

"Oh, yeah. But after a point it doesn't mean much. I get a lot more from my relationship with Clare than I do from my work. In fact, I found a use for my money. I give it to her school so they can buy things for the kids."

"That's good," Marika said, happy for her sister.

"So what's the situation with Jessica?"

"She dropped out of the program this spring."

"She did? Why?"

"I don't know why, but it's a pattern. She was doing well, and then for some reason she lost confidence in herself. And to make things worse, she keeps searching on the internet for someone who will fill the void in her heart and make her happy."

"I can understand that," Julia said, "though I wasn't searching on the internet. I was going to bars where women can meet each other."

"Is that how you met Clare?"

"No. I met her at the supermarket. She was looking for yeast to bake bread, and she couldn't find it. I knew where it was."

"Do you bake bread?"

"Oh, no. I just happened to notice it in the dairy section when I was buying eggs. God knows why it was in the dairy section."

"So that's how you met her?"

"Yeah," Julia said as if it was a blessing. "But going back to Jessica, I think Clare could help her."

"Well, maybe she could motivate her."

"Is that the problem? A lack of motivation?"

"There's motivation, but it doesn't persist. It comes and goes."

They sipped wine for a while in silence, and then Julia said: "So what about Nina?"

"She's fine. She has a good job at a magazine, and she has a serious relationship with a guy."

"That's good. Who's the guy?"

"The guy she's been living with for almost three years. And last week he finally made partner at his law firm, so now he should be in a position to get married."

"Then we could have a double wedding," Julia joked.

"That would be wild," Marika said, smiling.

At that point Jessica and Clare returned from their tour of the neighborhood, and after a while Marika drove her sister and Clare to the Yonkers train station, accompanied by Jessica.

On the way home she asked Jessica: "How was your tour?"

"It went well," Jessica said. "She asked a lot of questions about our family, and she was really interested. You know what I mean?"

"Yeah, I know." Marika had been impressed by the way Clare actually paid attention to what other people were saying.

"And guess what. She offered me a job at her school as soon as I complete my degree."

"That's great."

"So I'm going back to school this fall, and this time I won't let anything stop me," Jessica said with determination.

"You can do it," Marika told her.

"I know I can," Jessica said, gazing through the windshield ahead of them as if she could see it happening.

Marika gave thanks. Her faith was still challenged, but her hope was renewed, and her love was not only deepened but also widened. And she could imagine how everything might fall into place.

BOOK CLUB GUIDE TO

A Residue of Hope

Tom Milton

Introduction

Marika Bonetti is preparing dinner when she gets a phone call from the police informing her that the EMS has taken her daughter, Jessica, to the emergency room of the local hospital. Dropping everything, Marika drives to the hospital, where she learns that Jessica is in a coma from a drug overdose. Though her daughter has often gotten into trouble, Marika didn't know she was taking hard drugs, and she wonders where Jessica got the drug that has put her life in jeopardy. Marika's husband, Frank, arrives from his office as they're taking Jessica to the ICU, and they speculate that their daughter may have gotten the drug from a person she met on social media, where she's always searching for someone who will love her and make her happy. At the age of thirty-two, Jessica doesn't have a job that pays enough for her to live independently, she doesn't have a real social life, and she doesn't have the self-control to avoid repeatedly getting into trouble.

As Marika visits her daughter in the hospital and prays for her recovery, she wonders what she did wrong as a mother, and looking for an answer, she examines her life as far back as she can remember. Her mother and father came to America as refugees from Poland after World War II. Poland was devastated first by the Nazis and then by the Russians, who made it a colony of the Soviet Union. Her mother's father and brother were killed resisting the Nazis, and her sister was raped and killed by Russian soldiers. Her mother's mother had died a few years earlier from an untreated heart condition, so at the age of twenty she was living with a grandmother who convinced her she didn't have a future in Poland and connected her with an uncle and aunt who had gone to America before the war. With them as sponsors she came to Yonkers as a refugee, not knowing a word of English. Marika's father was raised in Gdańsk and trained as a mechanic in the shipyard there. His father was killed resisting the Nazis, and his mother was killed resisting the Russians. After hiding in the mountains from the Russians, he escaped to America and came to Yonkers as a refugee, sponsored by an uncle and aunt.

Marika's mother had a job cleaning the church and the rectory of St. Casimir, and she lived with her uncle and aunt, who owned an apartment building in a downtown neighborhood of Yonkers populated by Polish and Italian immigrants. Marika's father had a job at the carpet factory, which employed immigrants who didn't speak English. Her parents met at the Polish Center, and after dating for a few years they got married and moved into an apartment in the building owned by the uncle and aunt. By then her father had a job at Otis Elevator, working as an engineer.

Marika was born a year after her parents got married, and Julia was born three years later. From the beginning they were very different: Marika was happy being a girl, and Julia wished she had been a boy. Marika played with other girls, while Julia played with boys. Marika had a solid core of self-worth, while Julia had a void inside her and felt that their parents loved Marika more than her. There were also strains in their relationship because they had to share a bedroom, which Julia continually made a mess of and Marika cleaned up.

Though they went to the same schools and the same university, their paths diverged, with Marika majoring in English and working for a publishing company and Julia majoring in math and working for an investment bank as a member of a high-powered team that traded securities. Marika had a modest salary and lived in New York City with a roommate in a rent-controlled apartment while Julia made a lot of money and lived in a trendy neighborhood in her own apartment. During this period Marika was inspired by her first serious boyfriend, who taught English at Hunter College, to get a master's degree in English in the hope of someday becoming a teacher.

A year after breaking up with that boyfriend she met Frank in an exercise class, which she and her roommate took to stay in shape. The class was all women, but one evening it was disrupted by the appearance of a man. Marika was impressed by how well he did the exercises, and she was also attracted to him, but she thought he must be another instructor visiting the class to see how their instructor was doing, so she didn't expect to see him again. It turned out that he was a former marine with a degree in civil engineering, employed by a firm that did environmental impact statements for major developments. They started dating, and they developed a relationship that was based on the values they had in common.

They were married and living in Frank's five-floor walkup apartment on the Upper East Side when Marika's mother suddenly died of a heart problem like the one that had killed her grandmother. Since Marika's father depended entirely on her mother for his life outside of the family, she and Frank moved to Yonkers, where they could look after her father and start their own family. Marika got a job at a nearby college, teaching English, and after trying for a long time she finally got pregnant. The baby, Jessica, was difficult, and one of her first public actions was to swing her fist at the priest who was baptizing her. Three years later Marika had another baby, Nina, who was different from Jessica. Nina was a girly-girl with an interest in fashion, while Jessica was a tomboy with an interest in the martial arts. But unlike Marika and Julia, they had a good relationship, maybe because they never had to share a bedroom.

Jessica had an active mind and a generous heart, though she kept doing the same self-destructive things over and over. In college she started a program in nursing, did well, and then suddenly dropped out, explaining that she didn't feel she was capable of handling the courses, though she had done well in the hardest courses. She entered a nursing assistant program, did well, and got a job at the local hospital with the idea that she would resume the program in nursing, but she never did. Instead, she changed her major and earned a bachelor's degree in psychology, but she never looked for a job in that field. After several years she decided she wanted to be a teacher, so she entered a master's program in early childhood education and was doing well, though she was spending a lot of time on social media. By now it was clear that Jessica was looking for a woman, not a man, and that was okay with her parents. They just wanted her to be happy.

Shortly before the phone call from the police Marika learned that Jessica had stopped attending her courses in the master's program, and she couldn't understand why, after doing so well in the program for three semesters, and being so close to completing it, her daughter would quit. And now, with Jessica in the ICU after taking a drug overdose, she can't help feeling that as a mother she did something wrong.

A conversation with Tom Milton

Unlike most of your previous novels, which focus on social issues, this novel focuses on family issues. Why the change?

It's really not a change. My novels all focus on family issues as well as social issues, though in this one the emphasis is on family.

It examines the question that every mother must ask herself when her child gets into serious trouble: What did I do wrong? And that question is based on the premise that whatever the child does, her parents are responsible. But isn't that a false premise?

It's a questionable premise, which takes us back to the old debate of nature versus nurture.

In this situation the father, Frank, leans toward the nature theory, believing that their daughter, Jessica, was born the way she is, whereas the mother, Marika, leans toward the nurture theory, believing that Jessica's problems were caused by something that they as parents did or failed to do. And while she's praying for the recovery of her daughter, who is in a coma from taking a drug overdose, she examines her own life, looking for an answer to the question of what as a mother she did wrong. You've used this device in previous novels, with the main characters in a state of crisis reexamining their lives.

It's a literary device, but I think it happens in real life. At least in my own experience, when I'm in a state of crisis I reexamine my life or parts of it, trying to see how I got into such a predicament.

Well, as a writer, it enables you to develop a character in full, though you could also do that with a straightforward narrative.

I could, but I prefer to start a story in the middle and work back, and then forward.

That's what Homer did in his epics, so the people who listened to his stories must have liked it that way. But I noticed that while you were developing the main character in flashbacks, you were telling a story about immigrants.

A lot of stories set in America begin with immigrants.

Marika's parents are refugees from Poland, a country that plays a role in her life. In fact, in the flashbacks Marika is emotionally involved in the struggle of Poland to gain its independence from Russia.

Being Polish is a major part of her identity.

As well as her being from Yonkers. When she's asked who she is, she says she's a Polish girl from Yonkers.

She knows who she is, and she doesn't want to be anyone else.

In that respect she's different from her younger sister, Julia, who wants to be a boy. As a kid she hangs out with boys, and as an adult she works in a male-dominated industry.

Julia feels that her parents don't love her as much as they love Marika because she isn't what they wanted. She believes her father wanted a boy.

Could that be a reason why she wants to be a boy?

It could be, but maybe she was just born that way.

Julia measures her value by money, and she often talks about how much money she's making.

Julia is very competitive, whereas Marika isn't competitive.

I can't help wondering why these two girls, who have the same parents, are so different from each other.

It's the question Marika asks about her own daughters, Jessica and Nina. Why are they so different?

My mother asked that question about me and my sister. So maybe it's a universal question.

Whatever it is, I felt it was worth writing about.

Well, let's talk about Jessica, whose life is chaotic. Her therapist gave Marika a good image to describe her situation—a rotary for cars, where you have to get off at the right place in order to reach your destination. And for some reason Jessica keeps getting off the rotary at the wrong place.

Yes, that's a pattern of her behavior.

She keeps doing the same thing over and over, as if hoping for a different outcome. But isn't that a definition of insanity?

We've discussed this before, and I'm not sure if it's a definition of insanity, but it's a problem. The thing is, we don't know what Jessica is hoping for.

I guess we don't. We know what Marika is hoping for, what every mother is hoping for, that her child will be happy.

As Marika says in her consultation with Father Paul, at times Jessica *is* happy, especially when she's helping other people.

So her mother hopes she'll get into a profession where she can help other people, like nursing or teaching. But she keeps stopping short of the goal. Is it because she's detoured by the need for a relationship that she believes will make her happy?

She does seem to have the illusion that another person can make her happy.

And her use of social media is feeding that illusion. Which I think is an issue you're addressing.

Oh, yes. I've addressed it before, as I did in *The Godmother*. It's a major facilitator of Jessica's self-destructive behavior.

Her sister, Nina, explains to Marika that Jessica is "catfishing," or going on social media and pretending to be someone else in order to attract the person she's looking for.

Which always gets her into trouble. It's like going around the rotary and always getting off at the wrong place.

We feel the pain of it through her mother, who loves her and hopes she'll finally get off at the right place.

Marika has faith, hope, and love for her daughter. But her faith is challenged, and her hope is diminished. What keeps her going is her love.

You kept me in suspense about how this story would end. And I won't spoil it, but I think it was the right ending.

I must admit that I didn't know how it would end, but when I got there it felt right.

Well, thank you for another great story about real life.

Thank you for your comments and questions. They always help me understand things better.

Discussion questions

1. What do you think this novel is about?

2. How would you describe Marika as a person?

3. What kind of relationships did Marika have with her mother and her father?

4. What important values do her parents instill in Marika?

5. What is the role of Poland in her life?

6. How are Marika and her sister, Julia, different?

7. Why don't they have much of a relationship?

8. How was Marika's life influenced by her relationship with Thayer?

9. Describe the foundation of Marika's relationship with Frank.

10. What concerns does Marika have about Jessica from the beginning?

11. How is Jessica affected by her relationship with her grandfather?

12. What is the function of the subplot about Maggie?

13. What prompts Jessica to respond aggressively to boys?

14. Describe some things that Marika and Frank do in trying to help Jessica with her problems. To what extent are they successful?

15. How do social media play a role in Jessica's acts of self-destruction?

16. How might the issues in Jessica's life be resolved by the reappearance of Julia in the story?

17. Why might the relationship between Marika and Julia change?